WAR OF THE WOLVES

WAR OF THE WOLVES

(THE DEMON GATEKEEPER: BOOK ONE)

RUSSELL BROWN

www.blkdogpublishing.com

For Lewis. That was some walk in the woods.

CONTENTS

THE DARK MAN

Dressed in the colour of midnight, The Dark Man stood alone and smiled. Piercing red eyes, stared out through lank strands of black hair. Clouds of frosty breath whispered from grim lips. Fat droplets of water rolled over a grey face. Each one dropping slowly from a sharp chin. A ruby red tongue slowly licked moisture across stark white teeth. Sharp ears listened to the gasps of pain and fear echoing off the walls.

A jet of water arched gracefully upwards from the jagged teeth of a damaged toilet. A broken strip light swung softly, sending sparks of neon blue flashing across the floor. Cubical doors hung limply on hinges like broken arms. Cool water pooled across the tiled floor, mingling with blood and slowly turning the floor a rust colour. An air of menace circulated the room like a thick fog.

Through the settling chaos the creature remained still, a dark statue with arms spread out. His left hand extended into a silver blade that seemed to grow out of him like a wicked claw. Blood dripped from its tip and landed in the shallow pool surrounding him.

On the other side of the floor stood two men. Both were panting from recent exertions and both sported a multitude of sword cuts. They stood ready for battle, their arms outstretched, their eyes boring into the quiet opponent opposite.

"What are you against The Dark Man?" the creature whispered, the sound brushing across the floor like dry leaves on an Autumn pavement.

"I am the father of wolves, the mother of pain. You are nothing but playthings, a brief distraction."

The two figures growled deeply in response. Each taking a step back before crouching down onto their haunches. The sounds of breaking bones snapped across the room, followed by grunts of pain. Both men changed a deep shade of brown as course hair sprouted from their bodies. Snouts grew from their faces and sharp teeth protruded from their mouths. Their eyes turned yellow and their hands became massive paws ending in talons.

The Dark Man remained still, waiting for them to attack.

The first creature launched itself, its claws ready, its fangs flashing in the spitting light. A low growl erupted from its mouth, rising to a roar as it neared its prey. At the last moment, The Dark Man, casually stepped aside and brought the sword down onto the creature's exposed back. It let out a howl of pain and collapsed to the floor, sliding across the wet tiles and crashing into an empty cubical.

The second creature was more cautious. It stepped from one paw to the other, a deep growl of hatred vibrating from its chest.

"You are nothing," the Dark Man whispered. "You are an inferior breed. Come to me now and feel my blade."

The creature launched itself forward, teeth bared, talons deployed. Once again The Dark Man remained still as it rushed forward. Just before impact the creature fell to the floor and bowled into The Dark Man's legs, sending him clattering across the tiles. Before he could recover his opponent was up and rushing towards the exit, changing back into a human as it went.

The Dark Man stood up and surveyed the scene of carnage around him, the dead body of a man now added to the destruction.

"Round one to you, but this isn't a battle it's a war," he said to himself. He flicked the last droplets of blood from his sword and slowly walked out of the toilet, blue sparks following him as he went.

A COOL POOL AT MIDNIGHT

Lewis saw the wolf because he couldn't sleep.

He'd suffered from insomnia from an early age. His brain deciding to go into overdrive the minute his head hit the pillow. Arguments he'd had with friends or scenes from his favourite movie. That difficult maths equation he just couldn't get right, or the last line of that play he'd forgotten to memorize the day before. Nothing he did could stop it. He tried counting sheep, drinking warm milk and shoving his head under the pillow, but his mind whispered to him no matter what. After hours of turning and sighing he often gave up and went for a walk.

He knew he should stay in bed, but what else are you supposed to do when your brain won't switch off and you live in a bungalow on the edge of the woods? So he climbed out of his bedroom window and went wandering through the trees.

He wasn't afraid, these were his woods. He'd grown up in them, playing armies and knights, slaying a million bush shaped dragons and storming a thousand tree shaped castles. Now that he was older the trees were just trees but they were as familiar as family, and he enjoyed his quiet walks amongst them, safe in the knowledge he was the only human around. He loved the gentle creaking of the tree and the wind as it whispered through the grass. He could name most of the trees in the place and knew where each hollow and hidden stump lived. Most of all he loved the peace the wood gave him. It was the only thing that allowed his brain to slow down.

The wolf was crouched next to a silver coloured pool gently lapping at the water. It was the sound that alerted Lewis to its presence. At first his brain refused to compute what he was seeing, deciding instead that it was a large shaggy settee someone had abandoned in the woods. But the tongue darting in and out if its huge mouth and the gentle lapping sound as it drank water told him otherwise.

'What the hell is that?' He asked himself as he knelt down on the damp earth. He knew there were wolves in the woods, they'd come closer and closer to civilisation in recent years as the lure of easy food took hold. But he'd only ever seen their tracks. Now here was the biggest wolf in the whole world taking a drink at his pool, in his woods. Lewis liked to think of the woods as his, especially at night. The pool lay near its center and few people came here during the day never mind at midnight.

Taking a deep breath, he began to crawl closer, never taking his eyes off the drinking wolf as he crept forward. He knew he should be trying to get as far away as he could, But a part of him had to get a closer look, just to make sure that it was real.

His hands shuffled through a million pine needles as he crawled, the cold ground quickly turning his fingers blue. Water began to seep through his jeans but he carried on, eager to get a closer look.

As Lewis drew near the beast reared up onto its hind legs, a torrent of water cascading from its jaws. It stopped for a few seconds, balanced on its massive back paws, its snout lifted into the air, sniffing at the light breeze as its massive tongue darted in and out of its mouth. Then it dropped back down onto the ground with a thud.

Lewis stayed frozen to the spot. For a few terrifying seconds he'd been convinced the creature had smelt him and was about to come crashing forward, ready to snap him in two. But the thing had returned to gently lapping at the water again and he let out a sigh of relief.

He watched in fascination as the animal continued to drink its fill. Its fur had a strange silver tint and its head was surrounded by a large shaggy mane of black hair, that tapered down its back. Its whole body was covered in bulging muscles, that rippled as the creature rocked on its hind legs. There was a deep musk smell emanating from it, that reminded Lewis the woods after a heavy rain shower. But most of all it was its size that amazed him. He'd read about wolves in the wilds of America growing to be as big as a Great Dane, but this creature was the size of a small car.

Just as he was contemplating a safe retreat the creature reared up on its hind legs once again. This time it lifted its head and let out a howl before falling back down and clawing at the ground. Its body began to tremble, its skin bubbling like hot water. The fur on its back whispering with the movement. It let out a low whimper of pain and began to bite the earth. Ripping up great clods of grass and dirt that it tossed into the pool. It let out another howl and Lewis looked on in astonishment as the fur began to retreat and its paws morphed into hands and its snout retreated into its face. Deep yellow eyes suddenly turned black, then blue and lips appeared in the center of the creature's face. Its whimpering turned to moaning as legs appeared below a pink and naked torso. Within seconds a man lay where a massive wolf used to be, his head resting on his arms, his chest heaving as he breathed deeply.

The twig snapped loudly, startling them both. The man raised his head with a jerk and looked straight at the spot where Lewis was hiding. Despite the fact he was human a low growl escaped from his lips.

Lewis stopped moving. One hand in mid-air, the other hidden amongst the moss and pine needles. Half his brain told him there was no way he had just seen a wolf turn into a man, the other half screamed at him to run away. For a moment they stayed like that, stuck in a moment of fear and uncertainty, then the man got up and staggered towards him.

That broke the spell. Lewis scrambled up off the ground and began to race away from the pool. He ran in blind panic at first, sure that he would feel the creature's claws slice into his back at any moment. He ran around trees and over bushes, his face was whipped by branches and he stumbled to the ground more than once. He didn't care where he was going he only wanted to get away from the wolfman as quickly as he could. As the strength started to drain from him he slowed to a staggering jog, the cold air ripping through his chest like fire. He snatched a quick glance behind, half expecting to see the wolf tearing forward but all he saw was dark trees standing like silent witnesses, the wind gently speaking through their branches.

"That was real, I didn't imagine that," he muttered to himself.

"Hello!" he heard a voice shout from far away. Without a second thought Lewis turned on his heels and began to race through the woods once again.

Somehow he managed to stumbled onto the path that led to his home and stagger along it until he reached his house. He went around to the open window and climbed inside as quietly as his trembling body would let him, quickly closing and locking it afterwards.

He undressed quietly and dove under the covers, his body shaking in fear and dread. Every creak of a floor board, every drip of the tap sent shivers racing through his body. He told himself he was safe, that he'd gotten away, and besides he really hadn't seen what he'd seen. There was no way a wolf could turn into a man.

After a while he began to calm down and reached for his phone. He knew it was late, but he had to phone Charlie, she needed to hear this. After a few rings, a sleepy voice appeared on the other end of the line.

"Hello."

"Charlie it's me, I'm sorry to wake you but something's happened."

"Lewis? What's wrong?"

"Look you're never going to believe this but I've just seen a wolf in the woods."

"So, I see loads of them, they come into town all the time. They're looking for food."

"Yes, but I bet you never saw one of them change into a man?"

"What? Look Lewis, it's late and I have to get up early tomorrow. Just because you have trouble sleeping doesn't mean you can wake me up with your nonsense."

"I know this sounds like a wind up, but I'm telling you the truth. I saw a wolf in the middle of the woods and it turned into a man."

Charlie sighed down the line. "Give it up Lewis I'm not falling for it."

"I swear on my Mum's life, this isn't a wind up. Why would I wake you up with a story like this?"

"I don't know but I'm going back to sleep."

"I can't believe it myself, but I saw it."

"Thought you saw it. Maybe it was a bloke wearing a big shaggy coat and he took it off?"

"What! Howling at the same time and chomping on great big clumps of earth?" Lewis replied.

"He's probably a mentalist, the world's full of them, you remember Crazy Jean?"

"Yeah but this guy didn't chase buses he changed from a wolf into a bloke in front of me Charlie!" Lewis hissed.

There was silence down the other end of the line

"Are you telling the truth?"

"Yes! I can't believe it myself, my brain doesn't want to believe it but I saw him, and he saw me."

"What, he saw you?"

"Yeah but I turned and scarpered as soon as he did. I lost him in the woods."

"Yeah but he might come looking for you."

Lewis swallowed hard, he hadn't considered this.

"No," he said shakily. "He won't, he's probably racing over the Campsie Hills as we speak."

"Or he might be looking for the only witness to his secret. Why don't you come over here? My Gran's not here so we can talk."

"No it's OK, I'm knackered, I'm going to get some sleep, and besides I'd have to go out there to get to yours."

"Oh yeah, I forgot about that," Charlie replied laughing. "OK, meet me before class then, you have to tell me all about it."

"Yeah sure, usual place, night.

"Night."

Lewis pressed a button on his phone and everything went dark. He lay there for an age before dropping off into a fitful sleep, full of snapping jaws and eyes the colour of liquid gold.

FOR WHOM THE SCHOOL BELL TOLLS

The bell rang loudly, rattling through Lewis's head. He groaned at the sound and wished he'd gotten more than a few fitful hours of sleep. He'd just about managed to get through the day, with Charlie's help. He'd met her that morning as planned and they'd gone over what he'd seen the night before. He was convinced that a big part of her didn't believe him, and it surprised him just how much he needed to be believed. He'd intended to speak to his mum about it that morning, but she'd already gone when he awoke. Going over everything with Charlie had made him feel worse. It felt like he was telling a story even he didn't believe and her casual smirks and frequent questions only added to his frustration.

"Look, admit it, you don't believe me!" he had eventually shouted at her.

"Look I do believe you OK? I believe you believe you saw what you saw, but look at it from my point of view, it's a hell of a story," she replied calmly.

"You believed me last night."

"Yeah well I've slept since then."

"I saw what I saw. I wasn't sleep walking or anything, he definitely turned and he saw watching him."

She looked at him fiercely then let out a sigh. "I believe you, thousands wouldn't, but I do. So what do we do now?"

"Simple, we go and find evidence."

"Why?"

"I know what I saw, but I want to make sure I'm not mad and to prove to you I'm not mad. There has to be one hell of a lot of tracks around the pool."

"But what will that prove except that there was a really large wolf taking a drink?"

"He changed into a human, we can see if there's any other tracks, he wasn't wearing shoes."

"Oh I see, you mean we can see if both prints in the same place?"

"Exactly."

"Well OK I suppose that'll tell us something."

"It'll tell us I'm not totally mental at least."

The trip over to the woods was done in silence. Lewis was too nervous to speak and Charlie got that. They had to fight the horde of kids leaving school, then the cars and buses before walking down a million silent streets, each one as boring as the last. Lewis gave out a big sigh when they finally entered the woods and the familiar trees appeared before him.

The poolside was a real mess when they reached it. The area was full of churned up mud and grass. Large mounds of earth lay scattered around and paw prints and human foot prints clearly visible.

"See, I told you," Lewis said with a grin, sighing inside with relief.

"looks like one hell of a party."

"Nope just a great big man wolf."

"Do you think we can follow them?"

"Why?" Lewis asked skeptically.

"Well, they might lead to a lair or something. Imagine how famous we'd be if we discovered a massive wolf that turned into a bloke."

"We'd be dead, the thing would eat us whole," Lewis replied.

"Not necessarily, you said it turned into a bloke and he called after you. It might be totally normal when it's human, we might be able to speak with it and stuff. Besides if I can get a video of it changing we'll be rich!" Charlie said, smiling.

"Oh so that's why you want to go searching for it," Lewis laughed, "I guess you believe me now then?"

Charlie simply smiled in reply.

"OK but you go first!"

The tracks were easy to follow at first. As they got further into the woods it became more difficult until they were relying more on luck than skill. After a while Charlie stopped.

"It'll be dark soon," she said "I don't think we'll be able to follow them much further anyway."

"Yeah and it's getting cold, come on lets go to my house, It's Mac n Cheese Tuesday, want some?"

Charlie's mouth began to fill with silva at the sound of Mac n Cheese.

"Yeah lets go, we can come back tomorrow and try to find the tracks again if you like?"

"I'm not sure. I don't think we'll find them even if we wanted to," Lewis replied dubiously.

"OK, let's talk about it later, I'm starving!"

"OK, let's go," he replied, laughing.

They turned around and began to make their way back through the woods and had only gone a few steps before the sharp sound of branches snapping made them stop.

"Quickly, round here," Lewis hissed, dragging Charlie around the other side of a large bush.

The creature crashed through the undergrowth just as they disappeared. Lewis heard Charlie's quick intake of breath as the large wolf stopped in its tracks and began sniffing the air, much as it had done the night before. It looked around and focused on the bush they were hiding behind. After a few moments it let out a short bark and raced away. Charlie looked at Lewis and let out a sigh. "That was big."

They walked in silence until they reached the cottage. To Charlie's disappointment there was no Mac n Cheese. Lewis had to improvise with egg and chips. Afterwards, as Charlie lay on the couch gently rubbing her full belly, she contemplated what they'd seen.

"That was massive, but it was still a wolf."

"Yep, he must have changed back."

"Want to skip school tomorrow and go looking for it?"

"I'm not sure I want to find it or him, he could be really dangerous a total psycho."

"Are you afraid?"

"Of course, aren't you?"

"Yep," she admitted.

"The worst of it though is I don't think he'll give up, I think he'll keep going until he finds me. I saw something amazing, I bet he'll do anything to keep it a secret."

"Then we really do have to find him first and warn him that you're not on your own. It might be our only chance, especially if no one believes us about a wolf turning into a man."

"Yeah, he might leave me alone after that, maybe."

"So you believe me then?"

"I said so didn't I?"

The knock at the door was sharp and insistent. They both jumped up and stared at each other in fear.

"You expecting anyone?"

"Nope."

"Where's you're Mum?"

"I don't know, she's supposed to have been home by now. I'm going to give her a piece of my mind about dinner when she does get in."

"What do you want to do?"

Lewis swallowed hard and strode to the door. He opened it shakily and stared into the cold hard face of the man who could change into a wolf. His heart lurched in his chest, his hand froze to the door handle and his body stiffened under the man's intense gaze.

"We need to talk," the man said eventually.

At first Lewis didn't trust himself to speak, his mind screaming at him to slam the door in his face. He eventually managed to squeak out an invitation for the man to come in.

The man walked silently to the nearest seat and sat down. Lewis hesitated then sat down next to Charlie.

"What do you want?" he eventually managed to whisper.

The man looked at him and Charlie with cold eyes.

"Glad to see the gang's all here," he said cryptically. "I want to make sure you're OK it's as simple as that. You saw something extraordinary last night, something that you're probably doubting you even saw. I want to make sure you're OK."

"I know what I saw," Lewis said defensively.

"And what was that?" the man replied, looking at Charlie.

"I saw a wolf and it turned into you, that's what I saw."

"And who's going to believe that?" the man scoffed.

"I am," Charlie replied.

The man stared at them both for a moment. "No one will ever believe you, you must know that?"

"Then why are you here?"

"I feel bad, you saw me at my weakest last night and I chased after you. I feel terrible about that, I don't want to cause a fuss, I just want to make sure you're OK. I sleep walk you see and have terrible nightmares too, that's what you saw, a man sleep walking." he said heavily.

"I know what I saw and it wasn't you sleep walking. You were a wolf and then you changed into you, I wasn't sleep walking and you weren't either."

"Like I said no one's going to believe you," the man said after a pause. "Why don't you just forget what you saw and move on?"

Lewis licked his lips and leant forward slowly, levelling his gaze at the man's stony face.

"We're not going to say anything, you don't need to worry, like you said who's going to believe us anyway? We don't want any trouble."

"Except maybe a photo," Charlie whispered.

"Shhhh," Lewis replied.

The man's mobile phone rang suddenly, the tension broken by its insistent ringing. Without a word he jumped up and took the call, turning his back on Lewis and Charlie and walking to the far side of the room.

"Are you sure? They seem OK to me," they heard him whisper into the phone.

Charlie looked at Lewis and he shrugged in response. After a few more seconds of hushed conversation the man closed his phone and turned to face them.

"I believe you," he said with a sigh, "but that doesn't matter anymore. Regardless of what you will or won't say, things have changed. You're in real danger and I need you to follow me."

"Not likely!" Lewis said dismissively.

"You have no choice, you have to come with me now."

"Why do we?" Charlie asked.

"Because your lives are in danger."

"Yeah by you," Lewis said.

"No not by me, I'm trying to protect you."

"A minute ago you were trying to convince us that we never saw you change, now you're trying to save us, you're mental, that's the truth."

"Yeah well, most think that about me," he said laughing. "I can't leave you on your own anymore. You need to come with me."

"We don't have to go anywhere, but you do, get out of my house," Lewis replied with as much authority as he could muster.

"OK," the man replied with a sigh before opening his phone once again and dialing a number, "I think you'll want to take this," he said, handing the phone to Lewis.

Lewis took it reluctantly then listened to the voice on the other end, his face getting whiter as he did. He quietly gave the phone back to the man after a few minutes then turned to Charlie.

"We have to go with him," he said quietly.

"Why?" Charlie asked.

"Because my Mum says so."

WHO IS CALDER ROUGE?

Calder was cold, then again, he was always cold. He cursed his luck for being born Scottish. Not for the culture and bagpipes and all that, he was proud of those. No, he often cursed his luck because of the weather. Ten seasons in one day was not unusual in this part of the world, and today drizzle was steadily falling as he ventured outside his front door.

"Why wasn't I born in the Caribbean?" he often asked himself as he trudged through the rain. That was a normal refrain for Calder, that and 'how did I get myself into this mess?' he was asking himself that one more and more often lately.

The street was empty as he trudged down. The rain turning the pavement a shiny black. The only light came from a pale street lamp that flickered on and off at irregular intervals. He could feel the damp wriggle its way into his bones and he pulled his collar closer around his neck in a feeble attempt to stop it.

He'd been told to meet him here, under the flickering lamp, promptly at 11pm. Calder didn't want to be late, you didn't keep Mr. Mono waiting, yet here he was at 11.15pm and there was no sign of him.

"How did I get myself into this mess,' he whispered under his breath once again, as a drop of rain broke through his defenses and dribbled down the small of his back.

"You got into this mess because of love," a clipped voice responded.

Calder turned with a start and met the hard gaze of Mr. Mono.

"Isn't that always the way?" he asked. "Humans are weak but those in love are especially so."

"I guess you've never been in love then Mr. Mono?" Calder asked with a cheerfulness he didn't feel.

Mono simply stared at him in reply, his face an unreadable mask.

Calder hated Mono. He was a black hole that sucked all the light and joy out of the world. His manner was that of a newly minted robot and his emotions appeared to be none existent. Calder was secretly convinced that he wasn't a human at all and comments like the last one just reinforced his opinion.

"It's also what makes us strong you know," Calder said with a cough. "Yeah the best of us, love and all that."

Mono suddenly leaned in, his eye's inches from Calder's, their noses gently touching.

"Who is Calder Rough?" Mono asked. "Who is this man who speaks of love yet abandon's his wife and children? Is that love too Calder? Is that the best of us or the worst? I can't quite make that out can you help me?"

"It's the best of us," Calder replied, desperately trying to ignore the strong smell of copper emanating from Mono."

"The best?" Mono asked with a sneer.

"I do what you ask to protect them, that's true love. I'll do whatever I can to protect them. And I didn't abandon them, you took them."

"You'd do anything to protect them? Even betray us?" Mono asked blankly.

Calder hesitated a moment before replying, aware that his response could mean his death, or worse his family's.

"Betraying you would be the death of my family, I'm not that reckless Mr. Mono," he replied quietly.

Mono contemplated him coldly for a moment then stepped back.

"That I do believe," he said, reaching into his coat pocket and bringing out a piece of paper.

"You have proven yourself useful these past few weeks, I would strongly advise you continue to be so. Your information enabled us to narrow the search down to the estate you identified and our blood hounds have found the sweet smell of blood power. We are confident that this is the place but require you to interrogate further before we take any action." Mono said quickly before handing over the piece of paper. "We wouldn't want to arouse suspicions before we are ready to act so take care. We are in the end game and every step from now on is crucial. If you are identified we will take the hands from your little girl, do you understand?" Calder nodded mutely, fear rising in his stomach.

"What am I looking for exactly" he managed to ask.

"A boy, should be around 17, average height, slim build, brown hair."

"There are a million boys with that description, how can you be sure it's him?"

"That's what we need you for Calder, you know what you're looking for."

"But that means I have to get close, I might even have to speak with him. I'm no good at that, I'll mess it up. Why not just send in your soldiers and search for him that way."

"No, that would arose too much suspicion. We don't want to give our enemies any idea of what we are doing. So make sure you don't mess up," Mono said. "That would be very bad for you. Be here in three days, same time."

"Then I'm done?" Calder asked a little too desperately.

"That is not my decision to make, but I'll put in a good word," Mono replied with a shrug, before turning his back on Calder and walking away.

Calder shrank inside, fear and doubt overwhelming him. He was caught in a trap of his own making, his greed had led him to this, his passion for shiny things had put his family in danger and he couldn't see a way out. He knew The Dark Man would never let him go. All he could do was try to keep his family safe and hope for a miracle. Somehow, he still believed in them.

THE SHOP OF CURIOUS INCIDENTS

Lewis was confused, his Mum had told him two things, the guy's name was Bob and they needed to go with him right now, then she'd hung up. A million questions raced through his mind as he gave the phone back, how did his Mum know this Bob? Why was she happy for her son to go with a man who changed into a wolf? Did she know he could do that? If she did why had she never told him before? Who was his Mum?

They left in silence, another million unspoken questions racing across Charlie's face. After a few streets of walking she tugged hard at Lewis's sleeve.

"What the hell!" she whispered. Lewis shook his head in reply and hurried forward. He couldn't speak to anyone at that moment, he wasn't sure his mouth could form coherent words. His Mum knew about this guy, his Mum knew about wolves, these two thoughts raced each other around his head over and over again. After the initial shock of her command to 'go with Bob,' he'd felt numb, his mind had left his body and was walking meekly at his side, every action since then had been done on automatic. His limbs had moved of their own accord, separate and detached from his frozen brain. He'd drawn regular breaths and his arms had swung steadily at his sides, relying more on gravity than will.

"Lewis!" Charlie hissed in his ear. He shook his head again quickly, no sound escaping his lips.

"Where are we going?" Charlie asked, giving up on getting a response from her friend.

"We're going to see a guy who can help." Bob replied.

"Help with what, I didn't know we needed your help?"

"I'm sorry to say you do," Bob replied, "more than you know. I wish it wasn't like this but they're closing in. We have to get you away. You're in great danger, I didn't realize just how much until now."

"Until his Mum told you?"

"Yeah until she told me."

"What did she tell you? Why is Lewis in danger?"

"Not just Lewis, the both of you."

"Why are we both in danger?" Lewis asked, finally shaking off his shock.

"Mr. Blaine will explain," Bob replied.

"Who?" they asked simultaneously.

"The man we're going to see, the man who can help." Bob replied cryptically.

"And we're just supposed to accept that are we?" Charlie grunted. "You've more or less admitted that you change into a wolf and we're just expected to follow you because his Mum says so?"

"Yes and I don't change into a bloody wolf!"

"Oh come on, I saw you and you've kinda admitted it at least a dozen times," Lewis replied exasperated by Bob's replies.

"Lycan," he said "I'm a lycan not a wolf."

"A what?"

"A lycan, it's kind of like a wolf."

"Oh sure OK, just so we've got that sorted," Charlie replied with a snort."

"There's a big difference," Bob objected.

"It's all werewolf to me," Charlie laughed.

"Never that!" Bob barked, turning on her with hard eyes and thin lips, "I'm no bloody werewolf, you better get that one straight right now," he hissed through gritted teeth, jabbing a finger at her.

Charlie took a step back, her eyes wide, brows raised.

"I meant no offense," she said, raising he palms. "I don't believe a bloody word of any of it, you can be whatever you want," she said.

"What!" Lewis said, stung. "You told me you believed me!"

"Well yeah, but I need proof. You've got to admit this is all a bit weird? Some guy we've never met knocks on your door. He tells you he's not a wolf then changes his mind and says he is and that we're in danger and we have to go with him. I mean come on, I like a good thriller like anyone but this is just a bit out there, we'll find Aliens next."

"I saw him, and he's admitted it. My Mum was on the phone and said we both have to go with him. Yeah we need an explaination but it's real and it's happening."

She looked at them both carefully then shook her head.

"Good job I like a mystery," she said, "just tell me you have a car, I've been walking for ages."

"No car, we'll need to take the bus."

"Typical, you can bloody pay then, and you can get us something to drink."

They hopped on the bus, Charlie complaining that they had no drinks, and rode it into town. Bob seemed agitated as they were swallowed by the tall grey buildings, his gaze constantly scanning the streets the bus chugged along. He tensed as a man in a grey coat boarded and sat opposite them, but relaxed quickly when he watched him take out a sandwich and scoff it loudly.

"They'd never send someone looking like that," he muttered to himself under his breath.

"How do you know my Mum?" Lewis asked.

"I think your Mum should answer that one."

"Nope I think you should, you're here she isn't."

"It's a long story."

"Then start at the beginning."

"Let's just say I've known her for a long time."

"I know you know her, but how do you know her," Lewis pressed.

"We knew each other before you were born."

"And!" Lewis hissed.

"And that's it, speak to your Mum," Bob replied, turning to look out of the window.

Lewis huffed and turned away, his jaws clenching. "I would if I could but she's disappeared."

They travelled in silence until Bob jumped up and ran to the front of the bus as it started to pull away. He jumped off, quickly followed by Lewis and Charlie.

"Bloody hell you could have told us you were going to do that," Charlie complained.

"I needed to make sure no one's following us."

"Who would be following us?" Lewis asked.

"You'd be surprised."

"That guy's just weird," Charlie whispered as they started to walk down the street.

Lewis nodded in agreement. The whole thing was weird. He hoped Mr. Blaine explain it all to him, whoever he was.

'My mum knows him,' he told himself, feeling an acid burn race across his chest at the thought of his mum keeping secrets from him.

Lewis and his Mum had been close ever since his Dad had died. A tight unit doing everything in twos, the shopping, the cleaning, the cooking. They'd been practically inseparable since that day? He could still remember his Mum lying on her bed screaming into her pillow after the call had come through to tell her about the accident. She'd taken the news quietly until she'd put the phone back into its cradle then she'd walked zombie like to her bedroom. Lewis had been much younger then but knew that something was wrong. He'd called after her but she'd ignored him. He'd waited until he heard the muffled screams die down, then raced after her. She'd turned and taken him into a fierce embrace, rocking him back and forth as she wailed.

She never actually told him his Dad had died. But he hadn't needed to be told, the pain and lost on her face had told him everything. Since then he thought there'd been no secrets, the two musketeers his Mum had called them. Nothing coming between them, until now. It was the thought of his Mum keeping secrets all this time that hurt the most. He was even questioning his Dad's death now, had he really been killed in a car accident?

"We're here," Bob said, shaking Lewis out of his thoughts.

"Here? Charlie said. "This place is strange, I've been in it a couple of times. There's nothing but old rubbish in here and the boss is smelly. God this is a strange day," she cursed.

"Not everything is what it seems," was all Bob said before opening the door.

Lewis knew all about 'Hound's Emporium' everyone did. It'd been in this out of the way back alley for years. No one ever went in but it had a strange reputation all the same. One guy went in and swore he heard a chorus of babies singing, while another swore he saw the snout of a dragon peeping out from behind the back curtain, a tendril of smoke lazily curling from its nostril. One woman said she'd gone into buy a nice glass figurine for her

Gran and the proprietor had let several dance in front of her before she chose the one she wanted to buy, while another shopper had visited to buy a mechanical bird in a cage (one of the shops specialities) and come out with a real live parakeet they swore was a mechanical one, when they bought it. The shop didn't sell computer games, bikes or sports gear so most kids steered clear. After a while most adults did too, nicknaming the place 'The Shop of Curious Incidents' because of all the curious experiences customers had when they visited.

The door tinkled lightly as Bob opened it and they stepped through into a gloomy interior smelling of furniture polish and incense.

It took a moment for their eyes to get accustomed to the gloom and the contents of the room to reveal themselves. The shop was full to bursting with a million antiques of various shapes and sizes. Shelves were crammed full of lamps, statuettes, clocks, plates, jugs, vases, books and small boxes holding a million secrets. Large railway signs rested on the floor and painting of various colours and designs covered every inch of wall space. A large Grandfather clock filled one corner while a statue of a dog filled another. To Lewis's disappointment, none of them moved, and he couldn't see anything that looked like a dragon.

A small circular table, covered with a heavy cloth stood in the centre of the room. On top was a golden cage containing one of the shop's famous mechanical birds. It stared at them glassily before turning its head and chirping 'Hello'.

"What!" Charlie squeaked, stepping back.

"Relax it's not real," Bob said with a grin.

"Good afternoon Lewis, Charlie, Bob," a man said from the far end of the room. He was standing at the entrance to the back of the shop, a curtain held aside to reveal the room behind him crammed full with more antiques.

"I've been expecting you for quite some time."

Mr Blaine was tall and thin with a large forehead and deep set eyes. His shiny black hair was scraped back from his scalp and tied into a ponytail. A large ruby earring dangled from his left ear and a small trim goatee covered his chin. Overall Lewis though he had the look of a pretend pirate and tried not to laugh.

"Always remember we only see what we want to see Lewis," he said with a faint smile spreading across his lips.

"Mr. Blaine," Bob said with a nod before moving towards the door and turning his back to the room.

"Why don't we all have a nice cup of tea?" Blaine asked.

"Got any Irn Bru?" Charlie said.

"I'm sure I have some sickly sugary drink somewhere Charlie," he replied.

"How do you know who we are?" Lewis asked quietly.

"Because Bob phoned him stupid," Charlie huffed.

"I'm afraid I don't work with modern technology Charlie. A good question young man and one I will be more than happy to answer once we're settled, follow me please," he said, turning around and disappearing behind the curtain.

Lewis and Charlie followed him into the cramped space and sat down on piles of upturned books.

"Please forgive the state of the place, I just can't seem to throw anything away."

"Yeah no neither," Charlie replied absently, her gaze searching around the room's treasures.

"If there's something you see? Remember everything here is for sale and always at a reasonable price," Mr.

Blaine said as he produced a steaming tea pot from behind a stack of old magazines and began pouring into three cracked china tea cups.

"Yeah I bet," Charlie muttered under her breath.

"Now I suspect you are curious as to why you are here?" Mr Blaine said, pointedly ignoring her. "I'm sure it was quite a shock when you saw Mr Smith turn."

"Not half as much as finding out my Mum knows him," Lewis said.

"Ah yes your Mum, a very brave lady Lewis, she has protected you since you were a baby."

"Protected me from what?"

"Many things, but Charlie in particular," Blaine replied.

"Hang on what the hell are you talking about he don't need protecting from me?" Charlie grumbled.

"Please let me explain," Blaine said quietly, spreading his hands.

"You are both very special and you don't know it. That was deliberate, we wanted to give you as normal a life as possible and that meant keeping secrets, so I apologise for that to start with. When I say Lewis needs protecting from you what I really mean is kept away from you, but that obviously hasn't been possible as you got older."

"What are you talking about?"

"You're dangerous to each other."

"Why?" Charlie asked shaking her head.

"Royal blood power," Blaine replied.

"Royal blood what?"

"Royal blood power, I would have thought by now that you might have felt it but I can see from your blank faces that you haven't. You are both very special, you have blood power. It has been passed on by your parents and it's potent, very potent."

"This whack job's been hanging around with too many metal parrots Lewis, let's get out of here," Charlie said.

"I know it sounds crazy but let me ask you something Charlie, how do I look to you?"

"What?"

"My appearance, how do I look, it's a simple question?"

Charlie shook her head as she looked at him.

"Like a mentalist."

"But how do I look?" Blaine persisted.

"Like you was a thousand years old, long grey hair, grey Grandad trousers and braces, and you smell really bad."

""What are you talking about, he's got black hair and a goatee and can't be more than 40."

Blaine laughed quietly to himself as the two friends stared at each other incredulously.

"There are more things in heaven and earth Horacio than are dream't of in our philosophy. You see me as your mind wants to see me not as I really am, do I seem like a mentalist now Charlie!"

"Just because you're some kind of Derren Brown don't make you a Gandalf pal."

"I think I understand that," he said laughing. "But please hear me out that's all I ask. You are both children of the royal blood power, royalty in our world. Your families have this kind of blood power and it passes down from generation to generation through the ages. It can do many things, heal you quickly, give you great strength and even make you invisible when you need to be, it's the most potent type of blood power there is. Much more powerful than the normal kind lycans have."

"That's the thing Bob says he is?" Lewis asked.

"Yes he is, and so are the both of you."

"Next you'll be telling me I can change into a wolf too," Charlie said with a laugh.

"Yes that's exactly what you will be able to do when you have control of the blood power."

"You're telling me we're both Werewolves!" Charlie said laughing.

"No never that, they are our mortal enemies, I'm telling you that you are both Lycans."

"I've heard it all now, this guy's off his rocker. He's slipped us something in the tea, that's why we see him differently, let's get out of here."

Lewis didn't rely to Charlie's question, staring intently at Mr. Blaine instead.

"How can I believe you?" he eventually asked quietly.

"There's no way right now, you just need to trust me, proof I'm afraid will come later. Even if you don't believe me, I think you want to hear it all don't you, you have questions after all?"

"You're saying my mum's one of you?"

"No not one of me I'm a shifter, I can make people see me in different ways, your mum is like Bob, she's a lycan. But much more than that, if we had a queen then she would be it."

"You're a prince!" Charlie said laughing.

Lewis sucked in his breath and nodded, he knew that was the truth but for some reason didn't really feel anything, he suspected that would happen later.

"What about my parents?" Charlie asked quietly.

"They were very brave, they did everything they could to protect you, and yes they are royalty too" Blaine replied.

Charlie nodded, a single tear rolling down her cheek. Charlie's parents had been killed by a burglar when she was a toddler, she'd lived with her gran ever since.

"It wasn't a burglar what killed them was it?" she asked.

"No it was The Dark Man."

"Who?" Lewis asked.

"As I said werewolves are our mortal enemies, they are mindless brutes whose only purpose in life is to kill at their master's behest and their master is The Dark Man. All magical creatures have blood power running through their veins but royal blood power is very potent that's why you are in danger. He seeks you out to take your power. He's been seeking you out all your life and we've been protecting you. But as you grow older your powers grow too and it gets harder and harder to hide you and impossible to keep you apart. Imagine someone tuning in a radio, The Dark Man is trying to tune to you and the more music he hears, so to speak, the closer he gets."

"What will he do if he finds us?" Charlie asked, already knowing the answer.

"He'll kill you and take your power for himself. Then he will be uncontrollable, he will be able to create werewolves at will and will flood this world with them. Our world as we know it will end, does anyone want a Bakewell Tart?"

Lewis felt a sickening feeling in the pit of his stomach, it all seemed crazy but he believed it. He was in danger and his mum was too.

"I still don't understand how we're dangerous to each other," Charlie said.

"The power is doubled the closer you are to each other and so is the music if you like. When you're together it's like turning the volume up. It makes it easier for him to track you. To make matters worse you are attracted to each other like magnets, so you will inevitably end up being friends."

"This all sounds a bit Star Wars to me," Charlie said, but Lewis could see the belief sitting in her eyes.

"Whatever helps you get through the day," Blaine replied.

"Where's my mum and Charlie's gran?"

"And what the hell does my gran know about this, is she a lycan too?" Charlie asked.

"Yes, and she know the risks. We've all been living with them since you were born. Both your mum and your gran are where they have always been, ready."

"I need to speak to her, I need her to tell me this," Lewis said.

"And what's this about magical creatures?" Charlie asked.

"All in good time, we need to instigate the plan first."

"The plan?" they asked in unison.

THE PLAN

“It’s very simple, there is a key that unlocks your power, you find the key and you find the way to defeat The Dark Man.”

“The key?” Charlie asked sceptically. “Where is it, Hogwarts?”

“A good dose of healthy scepticism is welcome Charlie, but you need to set this aside now. I’m telling you the truth and you need to hear me. The key isn't a key, it’s sort of a gateway, an opening, a door. Well I don’t really know exactly what it is so we call it the key. It unlocks the powers you have, we need to find the key.”

“There’s a key that unlocks our power? Why can’t we just develop it? I mean if it’s in our blood we already have it, so we should be able to develop these powers as we grow older?”

"In normal times that's what would happen but we don't have the luxury of time, we need to accelerate your growth so we need the key."

"But you don't know what it is and I suppose you don't know where to find it."

"We're not sure exactly what it is but we do know where to find it."

"Where?" Charlie and Lewis asks in unison.

"In the garden of the night of course."

"Oh yeah the garden of the night, that's obvious", Charlie replied laughing.

"It's what we call the city after dark. It's our playground then, ours and the werewolves. We protect, they destroy, right under your noses. It's been this way for millennia."

"I can't believe I'm even listening to this," Charlie said with a sigh.

"Listening and believing, I see you Ms McQueen, I see through your sceptical words. You know what I say is true and you know you have a part in all this, the main part as it happens."

Charlie stared at him, her lips thin, but said nothing.

"What do we do in this garden of the night?" Lewis asked, eager to move on.

"I have no idea, that's what Bob's for."

"Hang on, I thought you were the Guru or something, I thought you had all the answers."

"My dear no one has all the answers, we have our expertise's, and field work is Bob's. He has an idea of where the key is, he's been out and about for years after all, I never venture out at night it's far too dangerous for me."

"Oh but it's fine for us!" Charlie huffed, "I thought we were royalty or something and needed protecting?"

"You do and this is the best way, have you never heard the saying 'the best form of defence is attack'?

"Have you never heard the saying 'never believe a smelly dude trying to tell you that you're a bloody werewolf'?

"Lycan," Lewis replied automatically.

"Whatever!" Charlie barked.

"I'm afraid you have no choice in this Charlie, your gran would agree with me. You are being chased and hiding isn't an option. We have to attack, we have to defeat The Dark Man, it's the only hope any of us have."

"What exactly is he?" Lewis asked.

"A demon in human form, it's a simple as that. He is from the nether world. A creature of infinite dark, an eater of souls, a consumer of spirits. His only aim is to eat this world and he will not stop, he has no compassion, he cannot be negotiated with. Our only hope is victory."

"Oh is that all," Charlie said.

"And the werewolves are these mindless creatures?"

"They are his creatures, bound souls doomed to obey him for all time. Every lycan destroyed gives him his power, but with the two of you he would have access to an enormous supply. He would be able to release the hounds of hell, destroying human kind in the process."

"So what you're saying is we're all that stands between this guy and the total destruction of the world?'

"Yes," Blaine said simply.

"No pressure then," Charlie said.

"When do we start?" Lewis asked?

"Right now, Bob, would you join us please?" Blaine shouted through the curtain.

Bob stuck his head through the opening then nodded.

"OK you two, follow me," he turned around without a backward glance and disappeared.

"Good luck to the both of you. I will see you when you are more enlightened as to your true destiny. Oh and when it's time for dinner of course."

"Yeah or when we're visiting you in the loony bin," Charlie muttered under her breath.

They followed Bob through another door and out into a wide yard, enclosed on all sides by a high brick wall.

"OK, now you know about the garden we need to go through a few things to prepare you before we go out."

"Prepare us for what?" Lewis asked.

"Anything, but mainly we need to prepare your defences."

"Hang on a minute, you were jumpy before we got here, I thought that was about keeping us safe, so what's changed so much now that we can go out again?" Charlie asked.

"You know about it all now and that's a big difference. It means I can show you stuff that will help to make you safe. I couldn't do that before you spoke to Blaine."

"Because it's that easy?"

"No but it's easier. OK stand apart from each other with your hands by your sides. If I heard right you don't have any feelings of your blood power is that true?" They both nodded. "OK this is going to feel really strange but bear with it. You'll feel weak and sick to your stomach at first but that will disappear quickly. Lewis close your eyes and picture Charlie in your mind. She's standing in front of you and she's got a great big knife in her hand. If you don't push her back she's going to carve her name into your stomach, can you see it?"

"Yeah that bits easy she's always wanted to do me in," Lewis said with a smile.

"Any more of that and I will go and get a knife."

"Concentrate. OK now you can see her in your mind imagine pushing her back, but not with your hands with you mind."

"What?" Lewis asked, opening his eyes to stare incredulously at Bob.

"Just bear with me Lewis, you can do this. It'll all make sense as soon as you do, I promise."

Lewis sighed and closed his eyes again. He saw Charlie standing there, a wide grin on her face, then he saw her begin to dance on the spot, her legs tapping on the floor, her arms waving in great big circles. He started to chuckle deep down in his gut but it rose quickly to escape out of his mouth. Within seconds he was doubling over, cramps starting in his stomach with the force of the laughter.

"What's so funny?"

"I'm sorry," he said after he got his laughter under control, "it's just that you're a bit funny in my head."

"Oh yeah ha, ha monster boy, come on, concentrate."

Lewis let out a few more chuckles, then settled down and closed his eyes. He saw Charlie and the knife immediately this time and imagined her rushing towards him with murder in her eyes. His mind emptied and his whole body became calm as the image rushed towards him. He suddenly felt weak and his stomach dropped as if he were riding a rollercoaster. His vision blurred and his hair tingled. A blast of energy rushed over his body. His flesh sizzled and his muscles vibrated. His eyes bulged in their sockets and his blood sang in his veins. The feeling radiated over his whole body before swirling into a vortex of power centring in his chest. It spun there for a brief second, a boiling mass of energy desperate to break free, before flashing out and hitting the imaginary Charlie, sending her rushing backwards across the yard.

Lewis opened his eyes to see Charlie rushing backwards across the floor, a cry of surprise and pain spilling from her.

"Charlie," he shouted, running towards her crumpling form.

"Yes!" Bob shouted exultantly, before rushing to join Lewis.

"Are you OK?" Lewis gasped as he fell to her side.

"What the hell?" Charlie moaned, sitting up and rubbing her shoulder. "What did you do to me? That was awesome!"

"Eh?"

"That was amazing. It felt like I was pushed by this great big hand. It pushed me back like I was a feather, I couldn't do anything, I couldn't stop it, it was amazing."

"Are you OK?" Bob asked.

"Yeah, that was incredible," she laughed, dragging herself up off the floor.

"I'm glad you liked it I guess" Lewis said, confused at her reaction to being thrown across the floor by an invisible force.

"It's real isn't it?" she asked, a smile of wonder spread across her face.

"Yes it's very real," Bob replied.

"OK my turn."

They practiced for an hour, each of them throwing their imaginary and real opponent across the floor several times. Charlie whooped and danced the first time she managed to throw Lewis, her face split with joy, gasping in great breaths and snorting through her nose.

"She's really lady like isn't she?" Bob said laughing.

"She's Charlie."

"Don't get me wrong, our greatest warriors are female. Its just that they aren't as full of joy at the thought of throwing an opponent."

"It's new, we'll get used to it."

"You'll have to. OK let's go and get some dinner, then we'll go out."

Bob took them to a small kitchen at the back of the shop and they eat a dinner of cold sandwiches and Irn Bru. Charlie talked through the whole meal, a million questions falling from her mouth.

"How far can we push people? Can we do other stuff like rip them apart with our minds? Can we jump over buildings? Can we fly? Can we really make ourselves invisible like Blaine said? Can I run as fast as Forrest Gump? When do I turn into a Lycan?"

"Bob had given grunts and one word answers to most of her questions but he stopped and looked at her when she asked the last one.

"I don't know," he replied eventually. "Only you can know that. You'll change when you're ready, that's normally when you really need to. When the danger is so great that you have no other options. Or when we find the key of course"

"Will it hurt?" Lewis asked.

"Yes, like nothing you've ever experienced before."

"OK what about this key?" Charlie asked, changing the subject quickly.

"I have a number of ideas about that. I've been doing research on it for years and it all comes back to a couple of places around the city. Old places and dangerous ones but that's where it will be most likely."

"What is it? Blaine didn't really know," Charlie asked.

"No one knows, but I have a theory that it's energy in its purest form. It'll accelerate your powers and help you change immediately. When that happens, you will have everything available to you."

"That's when we'll be able to defeat this dark guy?"

"Yes, you'll be powerful enough to defeat The Dark Man."

"Can't no one else beat him?"

"No, we can fight him but we don't have enough power to beat him and send him back to the nether world. Only you two can do that and you can only do it together."

"Best get started then," Lewis said with a confidence he didn't feel. "The quicker we find this key the quicker we defeat him."

They left the shop by the back door to avoid being seen and made their way along the alley, coming out onto a main street full of shoppers heading for home.

"Where are we going?" Lewis asked.

"Somewhere a bit quieter than here. There's still too many people and we don't want anyone to get hurt."

Lewis swallowed hard at the thought of the danger waiting for them. He looked around at all the shoppers rushing to finish their business and felt a sad detachment from it all. They led normal lives where they didn't have to know about Lycans and blood power. He envied their ignorance and wished he could go back 48 hours to a time when he was normal too.

'But you're not normal are you? You never were', a small voice said inside his head. He knew this was true. All of a sudden he felt a burning desire to see his Mum, to fall into her arms and hear her tell him it was all going to be OK. That he didn't need to go with Bob and try to find the key. He wanted to take a bath and get her to bring him crumpets and hot chocolate like she did every time he felt ill. He wanted to snuggle under his comfy duvet and sleep until all the memories of men changing into wolves had been erased. He sighed and shook his head. There was no going back now, the genie had been let out of the bottle and it could never be put back in. This was his life, he wasn't normal, at least not in the way most people on the planet knew it. He was a Lycan, a prince and the soon to be master of blood power, as soon as he found the key. He had to suck it up and get on with it. He could feel a faint tingling running over his skin as he brooded and guessed this was the first feelings of his power. It was more of a soft tickling sensation and nothing like the roar of power he'd felt when he first threw Charlie with his mind.

"Can you feel anything?" he asked Charlie in a whisper.

"Yeah I think so, I feel all tickly, how about you?"

"Yep me too, I guess this is it then."

"I guess it is."

They made their way along the busy streets, heading towards the outskirts of the city. They passed the Provost Lordship and the Cathedral, still full of tourists taking selfies, and entered a quieter street just behind. A worrying ache blossomed in the pit of Lewis's stomach as he saw what was in front of them.

"We're heading towards the Necropolis aren't we?" he asked the back of Bob's head.

"Yes, it's a good place to start looking. It'll be quiet at this time of day, it's ancient, one of the oldest parts of the city."

"Hang on that's a graveyard, I'm not going into a graveyard."

"You'll be fine Charlie, and you better get used to visiting creepy places, you'll be doing that a lot.

"Hang on I thought it was a Victorian graveyard, that's not ancient?" Lewis asked, ignoring Charlie.

"It is, but it's built on sacred ground that goes back to the druids. It's a place of power, it attracts lycans and werewolves, and all sorts of magical creatures. Like I said a good place to start."

They crossed over the Bridge of Sighs spanning the Molendinar Burn (the famous entrance to the Necropolis) and walked past the ornate gates and into the graveyard proper.

The Necropolis rose gently in front of them, the final resting place of some 50,000 souls, situated on a low hill just behind the city's cathedral. A thousand monuments stood in silent witness in front of them, most now shrouded in evening gloom.

"This is not good," Charlie whispered.

"What now?" Lewis asked, still ignoring Charlie's grumbles.

"This gives me the creeps you know that. I hate horror films."

"It's just a graveyard Charlie."

"Yeah just a graveyard. I bet we meet werewolves in here."

Lewis shivered at the thought, if they were anything like Bob, he wasn't looking forward to the encounter.

"Let's keep moving to the summit, I think we might find something there," Bob said, brushing past them.

They walked past a scattering of graves, turned grey in the evening gloom, and a large tomb topped with a weeping angel.

Charlie paused by a mausoleum built of sandstone with a large circular entrance. Built over what appeared to be two stories, a second circular level was topped with a conical roof, reminding her of the Chinese lanterns she'd seen in books. The building felt out of place amongst the ornate Victorian gravestones. It contained no inscription and had several grotesquely carved gargoyles over the entrance.

"That gives me the creeps even more than the rest does," she said.

"That's the mausoleum of Major Monteath," Bob informed them. "He was posted to India at the start of the 19th century, he wasn't a Lycan."

"Do you mean there are some buried in here?"

"Of course there are."

They made their way slowly up the winding paths cut into the side of the hill, the city spreading out behind them as they did. After a while Lewis stopped to catch his breath and sighed at the site of a million lights twinkling into existence below him.

"Beautiful isn't it?" Bob said.

"Well it would be if we weren't in the middle of a great big bloody graveyard," Charlie replied.

"Not much further."

They reached the summit of the hill a few minutes later and stood under a tall, thin column.

"Who's that on the top?" Charlie asked.

"John Knox" Bob replied.

"Now what?" Lewis asked anxiously.

"I'm not sure, I was hoping you'd be able to tell me?"

"Oh great, you haul us all the way up here at night and you don't even have a clue why. I thought we were looking for this key? Do we need to start digging or something? At least give us the impression you have a clue."

"Quiet!" Lewis hissed, his eyes suddenly locked on a small light flashing across the ground towards the edge of the hill. One second it was a bright white, then it turned lime green, then violet blue, then amber.

"I think there are some kids up here, they're flashing one of those pen lights," he said.

Bob followed his gaze and after a minute began to chuckle.

"They're kids all right but not of the human type."

The light was joined by another then a third and a fourth. Each one changing colour rapidly as they whizzed across the ground towards them.

"What are they?" Charlie asked, stepping back.

"Don't worry they're harmless. They're baby Sprites."

"Sprites?" Lewis and Charlie asked in unison.

"Ethereal beings,' Bob replied looking at their blank faces. "Don't you remember Mr. Blaine telling you that there are many things in this world you didn't know existed?"

"Well maybe," Charlie replied hesitantly, "he did say a lot of rubbish."

"Well rubbish or not it's the truth. There's a whole world of magic out there that your everyday person has ignored or convinced themselves doesn't exist. Thanks God they do. If everyone believed in magic and monsters the war would spill out onto the streets in the daytime."

"Real magic?" Lewis asked, watching the colours spin around each other on the floor.

"Well it's as good an explanation as any I guess. I'm sure there's a scientific explanation, something about splitting atoms and stuff but magic explains how I can turn into a lycan and how sprites can exist in this world. It doesn't let you change water into wine or pull a rabbit out of a hat. It's the stuff that keeps magical creatures bound to this earth."

"I never thought of it like that but I guess it makes sense," Charlie said.

"But how can I see them now?" Lewis asked.

"Because of your blood power. They can sense it's presence like any other magical creature. It's started to come alive ever since you practiced."

"You mean there are loads of stuff like this and we're some kind of cat nip to them!" Charlie asked, panic rising in her throat.

"No, I don't mean it like that. We all create a kind of magical atmosphere that creatures like this are attracted to. They won't harm you, Think of it like a moth attracted to a flame."

Charlie shivered at the thought of anything being attracted to the fumes she gave off but decided not to say anything. She was struggling to cope with the whole idea of werewolves, lycans and magic shops. Only yesterday she was a normal teenage girl, interested in make-up and ninja throwing knives and today she was some sort of twisted queen who attracted creatures of light just by sweating.

"What do I do if they come close?" she asked.

"They won't, they're quite timid actually, which is surprising considering how they are when they're grown up."

"What are they then?" Lewis asked.

"Bigger." Charlie replied with a chuckle.

"Yes and much more aggressive. We don't need to worry about that now, come on lets go back, there's nothing here."

They started to make their way down the north side of the hill but stopped abruptly when they heard a low growl coming from behind a large gravestone cut into the side of the path.

"Get behind me!" Bob hissed.

Charlie felt her heart lurch as the low growl turned into a snarl. She instinctively stepped behind Bob, shoving her hands into her coat pockets to stop them from shaking. She saw Lewis gently step aside, planting his feet firmly on the ground.

"Don't do anything stupid," she heard Bob whisper in front of her.

"No danger there," she responded.

Two ruby red eyes emerged from the shadows behind the gravestone. They were quickly joined by a wet snout and a cruel jaw, dripping with teeth.

Charlie instinctively drew in a breath, making a sharp whistling sound as she did. The hot eyes were suddenly on her, drawn to the sound she'd made. It growled low and long, emerging from the shadows to reveal a powerful torso and long front paws ending in wicked looking claws.

Charlie took an instinctive step back, her whole-body trembling with fear. She could see the monster in front of her and it was clearly a werewolf. The very thing they'd been talking about all day, but a part of her mind refused to acknowledge the fact.

"It isn't real, it isn't real," she began to whisper, taking another step backwards.

"Charlie!" Bob hissed. "Don't move another step."

But Charlie's mind no longer controlled her body. At that moment she was full of terror, full of disbelief, full of doubt and full of hatred for her own actions. She could no more control herself that a baby can control its crying when its hungry. She turned on her heels and ran as fast as she could.

The werewolf lifted itself onto its hind legs and sniffed the air quickly before bounding after her.

Bob scrabbled out of his coat, changing as he did. His skin shivered and wobbled, turning darker and darker before sprouting thick black hair. His arms and legs turned into powerful paws and his mouth grew a snout that ended in long, ivory coloured teeth. He howled once and rushed away after Charlie and the werewolf.

Lewis drew in a quick breath and stared around him, suddenly feeling very alone. With nothing better to do he rushed off after Bob.

A WORLD FULL OF MONSTERS

Charlie ran without thought. She ran without direction, she ran without hope, she ran with fear and a great big monster at her back.

Her lungs burned, her throat screamed, her skin sizzled and her calves ached, but she couldn't stop. If she stopped she'd be dead. She could hear the creature behind her, hear it growl and grunt. Hear its paws dig into the soft earth. Hear its teeth rattle in its massive jaws. She could almost feel its foul breath on her back and was sure drops of its saliva were dribbling down her spine. This spurred her on, helping her find the reserves of strength she needed to just stay ahead. She took in another lungful of air and skirted around a tall monument, hearing the creature smash into it with a grunt. She jumped over a gravestone, stumbling to her knees on the other side before hauling herself upright again and scrambling down a small path. She knew she was nearly spent and expected the creature's jaws to sink into her neck any moment. She circled around the lantern like monument she'd seen as they came up the hill, disappearing from the monster's sight for a few seconds. Grabbing the side of a column, she swung herself towards the back of the building, vainly hoping that the creature would miss her in the shadows as it rushed past.

She quickly snuggled into a small crevice between two columns, her chest burning with the effort of keeping in front of the werewolf. The creature rushed past her hiding place and bounded off down the hill. Charlie smiled as she saw it rush away from her, but it quickly turned into a grimace as she saw it skid to a halt and turn around. Its burning red eyes quickly picked her out and Charlie swallowed as she desperately tried to push herself further back into her hiding place. She was trapped.

The creature stopped for a moment, as if to catch its breath, then slowly made its way towards her. Charlie thought about rushing out and trying to get around the other side of the mausoleum, but she knew she'd never make it. She looked around her in the hope of seeing a spare tyre iron lying around on the ground but there was nothing but mud and grass.

The monster stopped a few meters away from her and sniffed the air tentatively, growling under its breath as it did. Charlie closed her eyes and waited for the inevitable attack, trying not to think about the creature's fangs sinking into her neck, or her warm blood soaking the front of her favorite Harley Davidson t-shirt.

She heard the creature's claws dig into the earth as it made its way slowly towards her, heard it growl and whine in anticipation of the impending meal, heard its nose snort as it smelt the air around its victim and smelt the moldy aroma if its fur as it came closer. This was it, she was going to get eaten by a creature most people thought of as a character in horror film. All she could hope was that it was quick and painless.

The creature tensed as it readied itself to pounce. That was the moment Bob (or the lycan formerly known as Bob), wheeled around the corner of the mausoleum and smashed into it with a thud. The shock vibrating into the ground and up through Charlie's feet.

She opened her eyes to see a mass of fur and teeth rolling away from her down the slope, smashing aside large granite gravestones as if they were made of polystyrene.

"Oh my God!" she gasped, sinking to her knees in relief, tears flooding down her cheeks.

The fight was brief, a flurry of fur became a spray of blood and a howl of pain, before the monster detached itself from Bob and ran away up the hill.

Lewis raced around the side of the mausoleum and skidded to a halt in front of Charlie. He fell to his knees and took her in his arms, concern written across his face.

"Are you OK?"

She could only nod in return.

"That was bloody close, I thought it had got you. Did you see the size of that thing? I know we've been talking about them all afternoon but I never thought it would be that big, I mean it's huge."

"OK you can stop talking now", Charlie managed to spurt out before crouching into a ball.

"Sorry", Lewis replied quietly.

They stayed like that for a few minutes. Lewis standing over her, not knowing what else to say or do, until Bob, the real Bob, slowly walked up the hill towards them. A large grin spread across his face as he pulled on his trousers.

"That was fun!" he said cheerfully.

"Fun!" Charlie spat from her position on the ground.

"That wasn't fun Bob, that was me nearly getting eaten by a mythical creature full of teeth and red eyes. I wouldn't say that was fun I would say that was terrifying!"

"Oh well yeah, sorry I can see it would have been a bit frightening for you, it was your first time and all that."

"Frightening? It was more than frightening, it was heart stopping that's what it was. I thought I was a gonna, I thought it was going to eat me, do you have any idea what that feels like?"

"Well yeah it happens to me quite a lot."

"Oh don't be so, so… Bob like", Charlie fumed, getting to her feet and stomping off down the hill.

"What did I say?" Bob asked, shrugging his shoulders.

They walked back into town in silence, Charlie still shaking inside and Lewis unsure of what to say. He wasn't sure how he felt either. He thought that seeing the monster would have awakened the blood power stirring inside him but it hadn't. He'd felt nothing but fear and Charlie had clearly felt the same. He wanted to ask her if she'd even had an inkling of the power but he was afraid she'd bite his head off, or worse, break into a flood of tears.

It was dark now and the town was full of orange glows and flashing neon signs. Despite rush hour being over there were still a million commuters making their way along grey pavements. Accompanied by the odd busker touting for coins and the stirring voice of a preacher trying to save Glaswegian souls.

Nothing's changed, Lewis thought. Despite his experience with the werewolf and Charlie fighting for her life, the city carried on. People still worried about getting home for their tea, groups of teenagers still queued to get into Fandango, the popular teenage disco and the Chicken Shak was still doing a roaring trade in 'burn your mouth off' spicy chicken burgers.

He would been one of those teenagers waiting to get into the disco only yesterday, but it all seemed so lame now. The world was full of monsters, there were werewolves, sprites and God knew what else. He was a royal monster with blood power that could end the world. There was a demon who wanted to kill him and his mum had been a secret lycan all his life. The world was upside down and he didn't know if it would ever be right again.

They arrived back at the shop and made their way into the back. Mr. Blain was making tea on a small hob, gently humming a tune to himself

"Did you enjoy your trip to the graveyard?" he asked without turning around.

"It was eventful," Lewis replied before plopping down onto a seat.

"Things will not happen overnight. Powers that have been sleeping since you were born take time to awaken. You have only learnt the truth today."

"You should have told us how dangerous it was going to be before you sent us out there," Charlie said. "I mean you knew we was going into a dangerous place and you weren't sure we'd be able to use any powers until we found this key. Which means we wouldn't be able to protect ourselves. That's sick, that's knowingly putting us into harm's way. I think there's a law against that?"

"Drink your tea it'll make you feel better Charlie."

"I don't want tea Mr. Blaine, I want answers!"

"I did tell you before you went out that it was dangerous Charlie. You are looking for the key in the garden of the night, there isn't much that's more dangerous than that. There was no guarantee that the blood power would help you and I guess I should have been clearer on that, so guilty as charged. It isn't enough to have a feeling of power. That's why you need to find the key, it will accelerate the process and give you the power you need. But if I know anything I know that it will be hidden in a dangerous place. I wish I could tell you something else. I wish I could hand it to you right now and tell you everything is going to be alright, but I can't. The world's a dangerous place full of dangerous creatures. You met one today. It will not be your last encounter, that is all I can promise you."

"I understand, but I still think you should have been clearer on all that."

"Understood. Now would anyone like a piece of Bakewell Tart?"

"Are there a lot of creatures out their Mr. Blaine? We saw something called a sprite but Bob told us there was many more things out there."

"Oh there's a whole world of creatures out there Lewis, Sprites, Banshee, Black Eyed Beings, Manticores, Wendigos, Unicorns, loads really. They exist in The Garden of the Night, a netherworld world within the human world. Most people choose to ignore them without even realizing it, their brains don't register the fact. Which is a good thing really as it would cause an awful mess if humans even learnt that they lived in a world where unicorns are real. Imagine the fuss that would cause!"

"Oh yeah imagine the fuss. They wouldn't be worried about werewolves eating them when they had My Little Pony to worry about."

"Exactly, it's far easier for everyone if humans believe they are the only important beings on this planet," Mr. Blaine replied, ignoring Charlie's sarcasm.

"A few hours ago I'd be calling the mental police on you, but I've seen them. I've seen sprites and a werewolf. I'm still trying to get my head around it, but it's real, it's all real," Charlie said, shaking her head and taking a large bite out of a slice of cake.

"Yes, it is. You've now taken the most important step, you believe."

"I thought I'd done that when I pushed Lewis back with my mind but the werewolf was a whole different world."

Lewis nodded his agreement. "Now what? I don't know about Charlie but I don't feel like going out there again tonight."

"Going back out again tonight? I'm never going back, I'm going home."

"Yes, go home. It's better if you have to keep things as normal as you can for now. If you go missing the authorities will ask questions and start looking for you. You're faces could end up on the news and you don't want that. Don't make it any easier for The Dark Man to learn who you are. We can't keep you hidden forever but we need to find the key, we need to accelerate your blood power, you need every chance you can get to defeat him."

"What if we can't find the key? What if he finds us before we have control over our powers?"

"One thing at a time, go home and get some sleep. Go to school, meet you friends, eat chips, do all the normal things you would do. Then come here tomorrow afternoon and we'll see what's what."

"Isn't home too dangerous now?"

"No, we still don't think they know where you live and you should do normal things for now. We've put a bunch of soldiers around your house and Bob will stay close to Charlie."

"OK, we'd best get going then," Lewis said, standing up. "Can you ask Bob to check what time the next bus is?"

"Oh after all you've been through I think we can do better than the next bus."

HOW DID I GET MYSELF INTO THIS MESS?

Calder shifted from one foot to the other and tried to shrink further into the bush. He'd been standing opposite the bungalow for 20 minutes and despite its isolation, was sure he'd been spotted by at least ten people. Curtains flickered, letter boxes flapped and the same car went past him three times. He'd found the address easily enough, even though Mr. Mono's writing resembled the binary language of computers. But there was nowhere to watch the front door without being seen from a million different windows. He'd have liked to have watched from the back, in the woods, where he wouldn't be seen. But he couldn't see anyone arriving if he did, so he stood in the street, feeling exposed. The bush he was trying to hide in was nestled against a garden fence but partially shrinking into its branches made him look even more suspicious.

"How did I get myself into this mess?" he grumbled to himself once again.

The car passed for the fourth time and Calder jumped out of his hiding place and began walking down the street. If his loitering in bushes alerted the police it would be a death sentence for his family. There was only one thing for it, he'd need to come back tomorrow morning and try to bump into the boy on his way to school. Just then the boy appeared out of nowhere and bumped into Calder.

"Oh sorry," the boy said as Calder stumbled backwards.

Calder looked up and was about to shout at the boy, when he noticed the air around his body shivered.

"My fault, my fault," he said, quickly recovering. "I didn't see you there sorry about that."

"Me too, I should have been looking where I was going," the boy replied.

"Oh well we'll know next time, won't we?" Calder said, laughing.

The space around the boy seemed to shimmer like a heat haze, as Calder stepped back to get a good look at him. He knew immediately that this was what he was looking for, this was the boy.

"Well yeah, I guess, anyway, sorry about that," the boy said, turning and walking towards the bungalow Calder had been scoping out.

Calder sighed and, stuffing his hands into his coat pockets, turned and began making his way along the pavement.

'So now what do I do?' he asked himself. He knew the sensible thing would be to wait until his rendezvous with Mr. Mono and tell him he'd found the boy. But then again when had Calder Rouge ever done the sensible thing? He'd fully intended to seek out Mono but that was before he'd met the boy and seen the power shimmering around his body. He now realised he had an advantage for the first time since he'd got himself into this mess. He knew something that Mono and his boss didn't, that the boy they were searching for was far more powerful than they could possibly imagine. His little voice was telling him to use it for all it was worth. Finally, he could see a way out for himself and his family. He had leverage and it was time to make it count.

Whistling his daughter's favourite tune about the gargoyle and the princess he made his way into Glasgow.

THE MASTER OF LOST PLACES

Derek loved abandoned places. He loved the smell of decay and rot and the grey/green mold that grew up damp walls. He loved broken stairs covered in worn out danger signs telling people not to enter. He loved the scrawls and graffiti of a million teen artists, and was particularly fond of the dripping sound that echoed across an abandoned subway station or long-forgotten warehouse. The sound was music to Derick's ears. It told him he'd found a special place. A space everyone else had forgotten, a space no one but him and his few friends wanted. He was king in this world. Monarch of all he could see, and quite a bit he couldn't, as most of the places he visited were dark.

Derek was the founder and chairman of Abandoned Glasgow, a society of like-minded souls, ten at the last count, who explored the forgotten by-ways of Scotland's greatest city. By day Derek was a mild-mannered shoe salesman, by night he was the Sultan of the Subway, the King of the Abandoned Abattoir, the Master of Lost Places.

He spent most of his spare time scrambling about in spaces most people wouldn't consider safe. Accompanied by his long-suffering girlfriend, Cindy, he would march around the halls of his forgotten kingdom, looking for strange treasures or forgotten art. Derek always took a memento of each trip into the lost world. He had a house full of lead pipes, broken tiles, ancient railway signs and curling posters. He was convinced it was all worth a fortune and one day he'd be recognized by the city fathers for all the work he'd done to protect Glasgow's history. Cindy on the other hand wasn't so sure.

One particularly cold evening, they decided at the last minute, to make a special trip into the lost world. It was ten years since they'd met across a crowded shoe shop, After Cindy had reminded Derek it was their anniversary they went somewhere special to mark the event. They decided to go to their favourite place, the old biscuit factory. Derek loved it because it had loads of old machinery and he could pick off bits for his collection. Cindy liked it because it wasn't as haunting as most of the spaces they usually visited.

They'd just gotten started when the problems began. First the flashlight went out, a real inconvenience when you're scrambling about in the dark. They'd just changed the batteries when Cindy realized she needed to pee really badly. With a sigh, Derek pointed her towards a small room on the edge of the factory floor.

"There's an old toilet in there I think. It doesn't flush but I'm sure the cleaners won't mind seeing as the place has been shut for ten years."

"I'll be back in a mo," Cindy squeaked as she shuffled away.

"Take your time I'm going to investigate the old ovens, they're fascinating. Did you know they used to bake
ten thousand biscuits a day in each of them?"

But Cindy hadn't heard, she was already disappearing into the toilet. With a shrug Derek walked over to the
first oven door. It was the size of a shed and smelt of ancient fat and burnt sugar. He took in a deep breath,
savouring the smells as they hit his nostrils, then hauled the
door open. It gave off a loud whine as years of rust broke
away, and slowly opened up like a gaping mouth. He was
about to peer into the gloom when something shot out,
missing his face by inches. He jerked his head back automatically and gave off a squeal of surprise. Lifting his
flashlight up in front of his face for protection, he waited
for more things to shoot out at him. After a few seconds of
quiet he lifted the flashlight away and tried to breath normally.

"What was that?" he said to no one in particular.

Swiveling around, he tried to see where the thing had
gone, but the warehouse was far too gloomy for him to
make out any detail.

"Must have been my imagination," he said with a
shrug and pointed the flashlight back into the oven's gaping hole.

They came out at him in a swarm of neon greens and
blues. A whirlwind of light that blasted out of the dark ov-
en and smashed into Derek with the intensity of a hammer
striking a nail. He was forced backwards and onto the
floor, the wind rushing out of his lungs as he hit the concrete with a thud.

The swarm of light engulfed him, turning his body
into a multi-coloured shape that writhed along the floor,
leaving neon smudges in its wake. With no air in his lungs
Derek wasn't able to cry out for help or plead for the
things to leave him alone. All he could do was churn about

on the floor in panicked jerking motions, as his brain screamed at him to get up and run.

Without thinking he shot out his right hand and grabbed one of the lights as they swarmed around him, squeezing down hard on the thing that struggled between his fingers.

The creature let out a wail of pain, and the swarm responded with a siren call of hurt that rang through Derek's brain.

Derek felt a million tiny needles begin to pierce his skin. His legs and arms became white hot with pain. His face and scalp became a mass of concentrated agony and his hands became numb as he repeatedly slapped them off the concrete floor.

He rolled over onto his back, in a desperate attempt to crush as many of the creatures as possible. They cracked and popped as he trapped them between his body and the floor, but the movement made his lungs burn even more as the lack of oxygen started to take effect.

With a monumental effort, he raised himself onto his hands and opened his mouth to try and draw in a breath of much needed air. As soon as he did the creatures stuffed themselves inside and tried to scramble down his throat. Coughing and choking, he fell back to the floor, his throat now tight with mythical creatures.

A part of Derek knew at that moment that he was going to die. He didn't know what the creatures where that attacked him and he didn't understand why they did. He just knew they would never stop until he was a lifeless corpse, rotting away on the floor of an abandoned factory.

Flashes of the collection he held at home splashed across Derek's brain as he struggled weakly on the floor. The image of a railway sign was quickly replaced by that of an old tin bath, then a cracked tile the colour of blood, then a pump, then a brass door knob. An image of Cindy popped into his brain and the creatures immediately lifted off him and flew into the air. The relief as a thousand needles stopped piercing his skin was immediate. He drew in a desperate breath, coughing up a few dead animals as he dry-heaved onto the floor. His lungs burned and his throat rang with pain. His limbs ached as the memory of the savage pain receded and his ears rang with the sound of a thousand fluttering wings.

Staring through a film of tears Derek watch as the creatures pulsed into the air, lifting up to the roof as a single angry cloud of magical menace, before swooping down and heading straight at a dazed Cindy, standing at the entrance to the toilet, her mouth wide open, her eyes bulging from their sockets.

They washed over her like a tidal wave, engulfing her in a myriad of neon colours that muted her screams of pain. She quickly became a cloud of light, boiling across the warehouse, glancing off ancient ovens and stumbling over broken bits of machinery in a desperate attempt to escape her attackers.

Derek watch from his place on the floor. The odd creature tumbled across his back or fluttered past his ear but he paid them no attention. His focus was entirely on the horrifying scene in front of him. At first, he was unable to get himself up off the floor, but he realised, as the pain and aching receded, that he didn't want to help Cindy. He was happy for the creatures to attack her rather than him. The revelation horrified him as much as the attack he was witnessing

"Cindy," he whimpered pathetically.

Derek had always been a coward. Worse than that he was an opinionated coward. The creation of Abandoned Glasgow had given him what every coward truly craves, power. But he was too weak to do anything with it, except bully the people around him. Cindy had been a longstanding beneficiary of Derek's bullying. He wasn't violent, but you can bully with words and looks just as well as you can with hands and fists.

"Oh I don't think the group logo should look like that Cindy, I mean I thought you were a trained artist but this logo is quite rubbish, not at all what we had in mind. Were you listening earlier? No, no your shoes quite clearly don't go with your scarf. I mean they're quite impractical and you don't want to embarrass me in front of the members, do you?"

Cindy had put up with all his comments and quirks without complaint. She sometimes wondered why she put up with him but then again where else was she ever going to get a hunk like him?

Her hunk was currently laid out on the floor trying to work out the easiest escape route. His girlfriend was now on the floor close to him, adding to the neon smears he'd made earlier. With an effort, his strained lungs complaining, Derek raised himself off the floor. He brushed the last of the dead creatures from his coat and took in another painful breath of air. With a final look at the multi-coloured mess writhing around on the floor he turned and made his way towards the exit.

"Derek!" Cindy groaned.

He turned with a whirl to see a Cindy shaped cloud stumbling towards him.

"Cindy!' Derek squealed, staggering backwards.

At that moment, the creatures doubled their attack and with a muffled scream Cindy staggered away from Derek, and made her way towards the opposite side of the warehouse.

He scuttled after her, his arms outstretch like a giant baby aching for its mother.

With rising panic, he realised Cindy was staggering towards the old lift shaft at the far end of the warehouse. The doors had long since been stolen, leaving a gaping hole in their place.

With an effort, his whole body still aching from the attack, Derek reached her as she approached the lip of the shaft. Without thinking he grabbed her flailing hands as she began to topple into the darkness, and tried to pull her back into the room. The creatures surrounding her immediately turn their attention to her savior, and Derek felt a million needles pierce his skin once again. With a squeal, he lets go of Cindy and she toppled away into the darkness, the creatures providing a neon glow as she made her way down.

At first Derek couldn't believe what had happened. Cindy made no sound as she disappeared and he didn't hear her hit the bottom of the shaft.

He cautiously lowered himself to the floor and gazed over the lip and into the darkness below. There was nothing to see. No neon glow, no magical creatures, no Cindy.

"Why on earth would you do that Cindy? Why would you leave me like that?"

When Cindy didn't answer, he got up off the floor and made his way towards the exit before the creatures could come back and reunite him with his girlfriend.

A RIDE IN THE DARK

Charlie groaned and rolled over onto her side. The dream had been real, too real. The teeth had been long and sharp, the breath hot and smelling of rotting flesh. The eyes had been hot coals of hatred, and the talons ivory coloured daggers of death.

She'd felt the teeth sink into her flesh and tried to shout out in her sleep, but the dream hadn't let her go. It'd clung onto her like glue. Pulling her deeper in as the teeth did their work. Tearing at her belly and chomping on her muscles. Pulling her tendons and snapping her bones. She'd thrashed and pulled at the eager wolf. Punching at its face and mouth, gouging at its eyes and pulling at its ears. She'd tried desperately to get it off her, to get it to stop eating. But it'd kept going, moving from her belly to her chest until it eventually reached her chin. It had raised its grizzly jaws and prepared to bite her in the face when she finally awoke with the bed clothes around her neck and tears streaming down her face.

She sat up and felt the room spin. Throwing her legs over the side of the bed, she placed her head between her knees and groaned.

"That was way too real," she whispered to herself. Then she remembered what had happened last night and shuddered some more.

After a few minutes of steady breathing, Charlie's heart began to slow and she stood up unsteadily, and went to the bathroom to splash cold water on her face.

She noticed her phone flashing when she returned and picked it up with some trepidation. The night before had left her feeling raw and vulnerable. She wasn't sure she could cope with another day like that.

The message on her phone was from Lewis asking her how she was doing.

'How am I doing?' she wondered to herself. If she was being honest she didn't have a clue. Everything she'd seen last night had been real but she wished it hadn't been. She wished she could go back to a simple life of school and home, with the odd trip to the shops thrown in. She was scared and unsure of what the future meant. Who she was, or thought she was, had been a lie. She wasn't that confident girl who could take on the world, while saving her friends from a life of boredom. After seeing the werewolf and realizing she was like it she knew she was a monster who only wanted to east human flesh. This revelation had rocked her to her core. She was something new, something horrible, something dangerous, something she didn't want to be.

She sat down on the bed with a sigh. "So how am I doing?" she asked the room.

'I'm OK, how are you?' she eventually replied.

"Fine, I'm outside your house.'

"Oh, God here we go again," Charlie mumbled, chucking the phone on the bed in disgust and reaching for her favourite black jeans. She dressed quickly, cleaned her teeth, brushed her hair in a desperate attempt to take some of the tangles out of it and finally put on lip salve. When she was halfway decent, or at least decent enough for boys not to notice, she grabbed her backpack and raced downstairs.

"Finally," Lewis said, "I thought you were going to take all day."

"I was considering it."

"Are you OK?"

"Why, don't I look OK?"

"Yeah, but you look tired."

"Well I didn't get too much sleep last night," she replied, trying not to think about the nightmare, "I was chased by a bloody werewolf you know."

"Sorry," Lewis replied quickly, "that would freak anyone out."

"You would think so," she replied sourly.

"What did your gran say when you got home?"

"She wasn't in. I never heard her come home now you mention it. She sometimes stays over at her friends when they play cards late. That's where she'll be.

"My mum wasn't in either. I wanted to talk to her about Bob and stuff too. It's not like her not to be home. Where's Bob by the way, I thought he was staying with you last night?"

"He did but he said he'd be leaving as soon as it got light. Do you think your mum not coming home is something to do with Bob and all this werewolf stuff?

Probably,"

"So we need to go back to the shop."

"Yep. We need to go and practice anyway, we're going out again later."

Charlie shuddered. "We're going back out again?"

"It's the only way we're going to find the key."

"Why do we have to look? Why can't Bob look for it and let us know when he's got it?" she asked grumpily.

"I don't think it works like that, we're the only ones that can get it, you remember what Mr. Blaine said?"

"Oh, I remember him. I don't know Lewis," she said, running fingers through her hair in frustration. "I just don't get all this. I mean I get it, we need to look for this key and we need to get our blood power up, I get that. But what's their role in this? Why are they so eager to let us go out there and get attacked by wolves? Why don't they protect us more?"

"They support us, that's what Bob does with the training and Mr. Blaine has been giving us advice. I thought you understood that from yesterday, why the questions?"

"I don't trust Blaine, I don't see why he's so keen on putting us in harm's way."

"We're not kids Charlie, and we put ourselves in harm's way. I don't know about you but I'm doing it to save my mum and the world, and I think Bob and Blaine have to do this. We're their royalty remember?"

"Yeah, I get all that, I'm just tired," Charlie replied guiltily. She'd forgotten about the saving the world problem, but knew deep down she had to do this for the same reason Lewis did.

"OK let's go."

"Hang on we have those invisible car things, we can take them."

Charlie shuddered at the thought. Blaine had told them it was a magical ride, but it had been terrifying to speed through the streets of the city on nothing but thin air. She'd been convinced she was going to die and had actually kissed the ground when the thing had dumped her outside her house, safe and well.

"No thanks I think I'll get the bus, but you go, I'll catch you up.

Lewis shook his head and laughed. "No problem, I'll see you at the shop."

Charlie arrived at the shop to sounds of arguing. Blaine was in a heated discussion with a man in a brown coat. The man was pointing his stubby figure at him and puffing out his beetroot coloured cheeks.

"Like I said to you before, it's your decision, but I'd make the right choice if I were you. Good day Mr. Blaine."

The man lifted his hat in farewell and bumped into Charlie in his eagerness to get out of the shop. Turning to look at her he frowned, before he exited the shop.

"That's rude," Charlie mumbled as he disappeared through the doorway.

"I'm afraid Calder has a lot on his mind," Blaine replied. "Good morning Charlie, how are you feeling after last night's encounter?"

"Just super," she replied sarcastically.

"That's what I thought. They're waiting for you in the yard. I think you'll find today just as interesting."

"Yeah cheers," Charlie replied absently before disappearing through the curtain and making her way to the yard.

Lewis was sliding across the floor on his back when she arrived, Bob laughing at him as he went.

"Oh dear, looks like you need more practice" Charlie said with a smile.

"So do you, what took you so long?"

"Bus got delayed by some roadworks."

"Typical, I told you to take the car."

"No chance, I wanted to keep my breakfast inside my stomach thank you very much."

"Not a fan of the car then?" Bob asked.

"It's not right, you shouldn't be able to travel by invisible car."

"I love it personally speaking but whatever gets you through the day," Bob replied with a grin.

"So, what are we up to? I normally get up late on Saturday, have brekkie watching the soaps and think about getting dressed around tea time. I guess that's not on the cards?"

"No, playtime's over I'm afraid. I need you to practice. Get a feeling for your power. You should start to get an inkling that its growing."

"Not sure about any inkling, but I did feel something yesterday."

"That's good," Bob replied eagerly.

"Yeah, then a bloody werewolf decided to try and eat me and I kind of lost it," Charlie said sulkily.

"We'll just have to try and get it back today," Bob replied, ignoring her mood.

They began to practice in the same way as yesterday. Lewis pushed Charlie with his mind and she returned the favour.

To her surprise, the soft buzzing of her blood power grew stronger as she mentally pushed at Lewis. At first it felt like a gentle vibration radiating out from her center. The more she pushed the harder the vibration got. After one particularly successful attempt to lift Lewis off his feet, the buzzing increased so much she could feel her bones rattle. It wasn't an annoying feeling either. It was more a reassurance that something was there that could protect her, an inner strength that she could release if she learnt how.

After a while Charlie realised she was enjoying herself and the horrors of the previous evening seemed like the distant memory of another, weaker person. She was surprised and a little frustrated when Bob eventually called a halt.

"I was enjoying that."

"Yeah, I could see, but you don't want to wear yourself out, you have a busy afternoon ahead of you."

"Why can't we just stay here and develop our powers this way?"

"Because that would take about a decade, we don't have time. We need to go out into the garden."

They discussed the coming night's activities over a lunch of sandwiches and tea. Charlie started to worry when she learnt where they were going.

"Underground? We're going underground?"

"I think it's as good a place as any to look for the key," Bob replied with a shrug.

"Yeah but underground. I mean we might get stuck or something. What about cave-ins?" she asked with a shiver. She hated being in enclosed spaces, preferring to see the sky. Black or blue didn't matter just as long as she was underneath it, and not a solid wall of rock.

"We'll be fine, there's no chance of any cave-ins. We're not going pot holing or mining for gold."

"Well not the normal kind of gold anyway," Lewis replied with a grin.

"Yeah exactly. We have to go to the places where the key is most likely hidden and the old Victoria station is a good place to look.

"What about magical creatures, will we see them?"

"Yes, they do tend to gather in places like that. Magical creatures gathered together away from humans."

"But we're humans?" Lewis said.

"Nope you're not. Sorry to disappoint you but you're lycans. You just haven't changed yet. But you could be mistaken for humans in a place like that, seeing as your blood power isn't fully developed, so we need to take care."

"This is all confusing," Lewis said with a shake of his head. "We have power and we don't have power. We might be mistaken for humans but we're not humans. If we don't have power yet how can The Dark Man get it from us?"

"There's nothing like blood power, and royal blood power is the strongest of all. It's in you and it will grow. He knows that and he also knows that you can give him a powerful supply, which is what you will have. It would also give you enough power to defeat him"

"So, we need to find the key?"

"Yes, we need to find the key, and soon."

Lewis felt weighed down by the responsibility of it all. Unlike Charlie, he'd quickly been able to accept what had happened to him over the past few days. He got that he was different and that he had blood power about to surge through him. He got that there was a world full of magical creatures right next door to the one he'd been living in. He got that some of those creatures wanted to kill him and everything that he loved. It was the fact that he was the only one who could stop them that terrified him. What if he failed to get his power? What if he failed to turn into a lycan? Worse of all what if he failed to kill The Dark Man? All these questions and more had rattled around in his brain since he'd learnt the truth. He wanted to speak to Charlie about them but she was clearly tackling her own demons. He would have liked to have talked to him mum, but she'd not been home. That thought suddenly generated yet another question.

"Hey Bob, have you seen my mum? She didn't come home last night."

"My gran didn't come home either," Charlie added.

"No I haven't spoken to your mum. I don't know about your gran Charlie, sorry."

"It's a bit dangerous don't you think? Not having our family at home when we get back from a hard night's work killing monsters."

"You're not out killing monsters and you're not alone when you get home. You know we have soldiers out there protecting you."

"But I might burn the house down making toast or something. Who's going to protect me from that?" Charlie asked.

"I'm sure you'll be fine. Besides, it's just a bit dangerous having your family around at the moment."

"Why?"

"Well, like I said, your power grows and it will eventually attract loads of other creatures, like The Dark Man. You need to get it under control."

"But my mum can protect me, you said that?"

"It's not your mum protecting you that he's worried about are you Bob?" Charlie asked through thin lips.

"What do you mean?"

"You want to protect her from him don't you."

"What, you can't be serious?"

"Well there is that too," Bob replied slowly.

"Why the hell would my mum need protecting from me."

"The power is strong and you need to contain it once it's up. But we can't take any risks. It's best if you turn in a controlled environment so to speak. The best thing is to have the people you love away from you when that happens."

Lewis still looked puzzled but Charlie was way ahead of him.

"In case we kill them, is that what you mean?"

Bob simply nodded in reply.

"I'm not going to kill my mum, whatever happens, I can't do that." Lewis said firmly.

"You think that but you can't control yourself when the blood power takes hold for the first time. It's like nothing on earth. Nothing anyone says can prepare you for it. The surge is incredible. A feeling of power like you've never felt and will never feel again. Nothing matters, nothing is important, nothing can stop you. All you care about is the feelings running through your veins. The power to do anything, change anything, kill anything. For a brief moment in time you will stop at nothing to get what you want, whatever that might be. Destroy a mountain, eat a herd of sheep, fell a demon. Anything you want is there for the taking, all you need to do is take a step forward and it will all be yours. If anyone steps in your way, they become dust." Bob swallowed and lowered his head. "It happens to us all the first time. You need to control that, to channel it, to put a protective wall around it. Anything to stop it taking you down and turning you into a dark man."

"Is that what happened to him? He became a demon, is that why he's so evil?"

"No one knows, but if it was, I can see how it happened. That's why you don't want your loved one's around you the first time. Believe me, no one wants that hurt. The feeling is immense but fleeting if you manage to return. If anything happens while you turn the only thing you'll be left with is the guilt, and that lasts a lifetime."

Bob sighed and stood up. "I need some fresh air. Finish your sandwiches, we're going out."

Charlie shuffled over to Lewis the moment Bob disappeared. "What do you think that was all about? I reckon he must have killed someone when he turned for the first time. I bet it was his wife or mum or something. That must have been awful. I don't want that to happened to us. He's right, it's best if our families are nowhere near us the first time we turn."

"I don't care what happened to him, there's no way I could hurt my mum, no matter what I was feeling or how much blood power is going through me," he said firmly.

"I hope you're right, but remember what he said? No one can prepare you for that. I'm not sure I want those feelings, I think I'd rather go home and hide under the duvet."

"We don't have a choice. It's us or them. We have to defeat The Dark Man, otherwise the world's toast."

"What if he doesn't exist? What if this is just an elaborate hoax to get us to change so they can feed on our power? Ever thought about that?"

"I have, but I don't think they're suspicious like you do.

"I just hope you're right."

They went outside to join Bob. It was a bright winter's afternoon. The low sun spread soft heat across their faces and warmed their skin. The gentle hum of a thousand pedestrians vibrated in the air and Charlie caught herself wishing she was one of them once again.

"I wonder if my Gran's started the Christmas shopping yet?' she mused idly.

"Yeah, she's getting you that key you always wanted," Lewis replied with a grin.

"Oh ha, ha, very funny, you should be on the stage."

"OK let's go," Bob said his face cold and determined.

"You OK Bob?"

"Me? I'm fine. Look we're going somewhere different tonight. It's not like the grave yard."

"Oh, yeah it's way nicer, it'll have its own cave-in and everything," Charlie interrupted.

"You'll be fine Charlie," Bob said patiently, "just follow my lead. We're going to a place where there'll be more creatures than yesterday so keep your wits about you and do everything I say."

They both nodded their agreement.

Bob took them back through the shop and out into the yard. He kept on walking and a gate appeared in the back wall as he approached it. A gate that hadn't been there only moments before.

"What's this?" Charlie asked suspiciously.

"Relax it's always been there you just didn't notice it before."

They walked through and into a grey back alley full of bins and weeds.

Bob reached into his pocket and took out what looked like seeds. He rolled them around in his palm before lifting them to his lips and blowing them gently into the air. They wheeled around in front of him for a few seconds before slowly dissolving.

"Here," he said, reaching into his pocket and taking out more seeds. "Take some of these each. If you get into bother blow these into the air and help will come."

"What kind of help?" Lewis asked.

"The kind that gets you out of a sticky situation."

The seeds felt heavy in Lewis's palm, more like ball bearings than seeds. He rolled them around his hand, watching them change colour as he did, before carefully dropping them into his pocket.

After a few quiet moments, the earth beneath their feet began to hum gently, shifting crisp packets and sweet rappers across the path.

"What's that?" Charlie asked nervously.

"Our ride," Bob replied casually.

A grate at the side of the alley began to moan and grind. The metal expanded over the ground, pushing weeds and waste in its wake. It slowly grew in size, the moaning and grinding growing steadily louder as it did.

"What is that?" Charlie asked, stumbling away from the growing hole.

"Relax it's perfectly normal," Bob replied.

"A great big hole opening up in front of you is not normal."

"It is in our world."

The grate stopped expanding after a few more screeches and groans. Then it gently opened up.

"OK let's go," Bob said, stepping into the grate and disappearing into the darkness.

Charlie swallowed hard and nodded for Lewis to follow Bob.

"I'll follow you don't worry."

"I'm sure it's fine, he wouldn't put us in danger."

"Don't worry I just need a second that's all. I'll be right behind you."

She watched as Lewis disappeared, then tentatively stepped towards the grate.

"It's fine, it's nothing but a door, that's all," she reassured herself.

"Are you coming?" a voice asked from the darkness.

"On my way," Charlie responded with a confidence she didn't feel.

Now she was close to the entrance she could see that there was a series of steps leading down into the darkness. She put her foot tentatively onto the first one and waited for something to happen. When nothing did she took a deep breath, and stepped down into the hole.

The dark enveloped her quickly but the steps began to glow as she made her way down and she was able to see her way to the bottom easily. They led out into a large corridor, lit by an earie green light.

"OK, this is the chute."

"The what?"

"The chute, it's like an underground railway. It's our way of getting around underground quickly. Those seeds I gave you are a way of calling to it. If you release them it'll come to you wherever you are."

"Wherever?"

"Yep, anywhere. If you're in trouble it's a great way of getting out. Used it to get out of a few tricky situations in my time. For now, it's going to take us where we need to be, and don't worry Charlie it's not invisible."

"But where is it?"

"There," Bob replied, pointing to the opposite side of the corridor. The lights suddenly flared to reveal a sleek silver coloured shape sitting on two brass coloured rails. It reminded Lewis of a large bullet resting on its side. With a loud click the side of the chute opened up to reveal a plush red interior with three seats sitting one behind the other.

"That's different," Lewis said.

"It's the best way I know of getting around under the city, and it's free."

"What about the invisible car thing?"

"That doesn't work underground, no idea why."

They stepped forward and took a seat each. Bob took the front one and began to push on neon blue buttons set in a console in front of him.

"It won't take long for us to get to Victoria station in this, but you'll need to make sure your seatbelts are nice and tight. This thing is fast. With that he pressed a large button with the word 'close' displayed on it and the chute closed tight.

Charlie drew in a nervous breath as the world went dark. For a moment, she was terrified they were going to go bouncing around underground in the dark, then blue neon lights appeared, giving the interior a strange greenish glow. The chute lurched forward, throwing them all back into their chairs. Charlie closed her eyes tight and clamped her mouth shut. The chute began to lurch left and right, seeming to gain speed as it did.

'Another bloody ride in the dark!' Charlie groaned, trying to sink back into her chair as far as she could go.

ZANDER HEART

Zander Heart was in love. She'd never admit it to anyone, especially the person she was in love with, but she was and she knew it. She wasn't happy about it either. It was very inconvenient. The one thing you didn't need in her line of work was emotion, it made you weak. Despite her name, Zander was known for being as hard as nails. She wasn't all heart, she was no heart. You couldn't afford any weaknesses when you were spending every day fighting for your life.

Zander was a soldier. A Lycan soldier to be exact. She was one of the elite, the few, the thin red line between chaos and peace. She didn't have time for a private life, especially one that included love. Her job was all consuming. It had to be when you were putting your life on the line and expecting your comrades to do the same.

So, it had come as a surprise when she realized she was in love. It wasn't what she'd been expecting and certainly not what she'd been looking for.

One day she was happily killing werewolves for a living, the next she was experiencing the heart wrenching, gut churning, pain of passionate love.

She'd considered talking to someone about it. Not an easy thing for a soldier who was used to covering up their feelings. Then she realised there was no one she could talk to anyway. Bob was a non-starter, he'd tell everyone else. She didn't trust Blaine and she wasn't very fond of her fellow troopers, especially Curly who she despised and Martine who she considered an idiot. So, she bottled it up, letting the pain and the heartache increase. Letting it eat at her until she couldn't eat and she couldn't sleep and she couldn't concentrate on anything but the amazing blue eyes and full red lips of the women she loved.

Zander didn't have a family. Her mum and dad had died when she was very young and she'd grown up in one care home after another. She'd stay in one place for a few months, then something would go wrong. Usually she was the cause, and she was quietly moved to another house or another orphanage until something went wrong there and she was moved on again.

It meant that she never really got to make friends. Everyone she met had a frown. That was until Mr. Blaine visited her. He was different. He smiled at her for a start and actually spoke to her like an equal, something she found unnerving at first. He told her about lycans and werewolves and explained the difference. He told her about her mum and dad, and how they'd been lycans. Finally, he told her about herself. He explained all about the pain and loss she didn't even know she was feeling and he told her she was a lycan too. From then on Zander had been a soldier. She'd seen combat in most parts of the world and gained a reputation for being as hard as nails.

There were rumours she even took on a group of werewolves on her own once.

But she'd been distant with the other soldiers from the start. Not really sure how to deal with a group of happy, joking people, she'd withdrawn into herself and been there ever since. That was until she'd finally realised she was in love. That had made things worse. Now she didn't know how to act in front of her, or what to say.

The werewolf's paw came down at speed and missed her face by inches, sending thoughts of love and full red lips spinning from her mind. Zander felt the hot glow of change rise up from the pit of her stomach and within seconds she was a snarling, biting lycan.

She turned to see the werewolf charging towards her and smiled. This was going to be fun. With a roar, she dug her massive paws into the soft earth and launched her body at the beast. The power rushing through her at that moment was intoxicating. Zander had never really gotten used to the feelings of being a powerful lycan. During her first time, she was certain it would split her apart as the blood power roared through her veins. But she'd survived, just, and slowly managed to understand the immense power she'd been given. Now she channeled her rage at her enemies. Focusing all her power on destroying the werewolf trying to destroy her.

They met in the middle of a misty field. The power of the collision ripping through the air like a thunder clap. In a few seconds, Zander had gained a hold on the werewolf's throat and was bounding around the field with it in her mouth. She danced over the muddy earth like a puppy playing with its favourite toy. Flinging the body up into the air and trying to catch it with her paws on the way down. The thrill of the victory and the hot, metal taste of blood in her mouth was intoxicating. She never got used to it no matter how many times it happened. She carried on playing with her prey until she realised the rest of her crew were warily watching her. Something was wrong. The field, a scene of vicious fighting only moments before, had become quiet.

She dropped her limp toy and looked around. There were numerous dead littered across the ground. Lycans stood in-between them breathing deeply. One or two were changing back into human form. Pale, twisting lumps of flesh, shining in the white light.

Zander took a deep breath and started her usual routine of scanning the faces of lycans and humans. She was a soldier and she needed to make sure her comrades were OK. That was what she told herself, and it would have been true until recently. Now she was looking to make sure the love of her life was OK, and she was getting worried, she couldn't see her standing or turning.

Without thinking she began to pace around the field, looking into each pale face as she did. Halfway across she turned back into a human, continuing her desperate search without pause.

Suddenly Curly appeared in front of her, his face a mask of concern.

"What?" Zander asked distractedly.

"It's Lila, Zan, I think she's really hurt."

The words hit Zander like a hammer blow. At first, she didn't know how to react. Curly was telling her something about Lila, about her love, but it couldn't possibly be right. Lila was a warrior, she was a Lycan champion, survivor of a million battles. She never got hurt. Zander couldn't remember her ever having a scratch. Until now, until she'd become the love of her life.

"What do you mean she's really hurt?' she managed to croak.

"I think you better come and look for yourself."

They trudged across the field without a word, the mist curling around their feet. As they drew near to the edge of the field, Zander could make out a twisted form, mostly hidden by the fog. At first it was just a shape, then a leg and a hand appeared, and Zander's heart stopped. The colour of the nails, bright orange, was unmistakably Lila's.

"No!", Zander barked, rushing towards Lila's silent form. "No, no, no, what the hell have you done, what the hell have you done," she repeated over and over, placing one hand gently on Lila's shoulder. Hot salty tears tumbled down her cheeks and landed on the cold, pale form below her. It was the first time she'd cried since her mum and dad had been killed. Zander was no longer as hard as nails.

Her brain wouldn't accept that it was Lila laying there. It told her it was someone else, maybe even a were-wolf that looked like her and wore the same colour nail varnish.

It couldn't be Lila, she was loved, she was needed, she had a future ahead of her, a future that included Zander and maybe a few kittens. She was a warrior who never got cut, never got caught. She'd been in a thousand battles and come out the other end laughing. Apart from Zander she had the most skill, the most power and the most victories. It couldn't be Lila, it had to be someone else.

"We have to get her back to Blaine, Zan. He'll want to perform the ceremony."

"Ceremony?" Zander choked through a vale of tears.

"Yeah, we have to say goodbye, he'll want to honour her blood power."

"No!" she screamed. "No one's touching her, no one's taking anything from her, got it!"

Curly stepped back and quickly nodded, "OK."

Zander took the still form in her arms and wept. She wailed, she cried, she screamed at the dark sky, while her fellow lycans stood around her and in unison, wailed at the moon.

At the far end of the field, shrouded by dark trees, a figure with eyes the colour of hot rubies, watched and smiled.

VICTORIA STATION

The speeding bullet came to a sudden stop, sending Lewis lurching out of his seat.

"You could have given us a warning," Charlie mumbled behind him.

"Sorry about that, you'll get used to it. Wasn't that fun?."

"I'm not sure I'd say that, but it was better than the invisible car."

"OK listen up. This is going to be different from the cemetery. There's a lot more creatures down here and some of them aren't friendly. You'll need your wits about you and your eyes peeled. Stay close to me and do everything I say. If we get into trouble use the grains I gave you and get out of dodge, clear?" they both nodded. "Good, let's have fun."

"Fun, is that what you call it?"

"Come on Charlie, this will be a laugh. If you can't laugh in the face of death when can you?"

"You're a scream Bob, a real joker."

"True," Bob replied with a shrug.

"So, what are we looking for?" Lewis asked.

"Same as before, you'll know it when you see it."

"We're just going to generally stroll about then?"

"More or less. Oh, we're going to have a chat with The Gatherer too."

"The who?"

"The Gatherer. Hasn't Blaine told you about him?"

"No, who is he?"

"He's the guy that lives in the station."

"We're going into an abandoned underground station to talk to someone called The Gatherer, of course we know all about that."

"No need to be so sarcastic Charlie. He's very old. No one knows how old. Been down here for ages. We need info on The Dark Man and The Gatherer can help."

"Will he know where we can find the key?"

"No, I wish he did. We would have come here yesterday instead of wasting our time up at the Necropolis. He gathers info on most things, but he can't help with that. Besides we don't really want to ask. He's not what you would call a friend. He'll help anyone for gold, lycan, werewolf, it doesn't matter to him. He's not on anyone's side, so best not tell him something as important as that, just in case someone comes along with more gold and asks about us, if you know what I mean?"

"What do you need to know about The Dark Man?"

"Where his lair is."

"Haven't you asked about that until now?"

"Of course we have, but he moves about a lot, so we need to keep searching."

"What are you going to do if you find out?"

"Pay him a visit."

"It's as easy as that. You pay this Gatherer and he tells you where the enemy is?"

"No of course not, we just think he might know. It's worth a try at least."

"What'll you do if he tells you where he is and you pay him a visit?"

Bob looked at them both coldly and said nothing.

"Oh, I see."

"What's stopping this guy telling The Dark Man where we are then?"

"He'd have to know who you are first and seeing as he doesn't he can't really ask where you live."

"I suppose so."

"Right, stay close."

They set off down a damp tunnel smelling of rotting rubbish and decaying bodies. The ground was wet and slimy and the sound of dripping water was everywhere.

"Something's died down here, can you smell it?" Charlie asked.

"Lots of things have died down here."

Charlie tried not to think about what had died in the dark, concentrating instead on following Bob and his flashlight. After a few hundred meters, they could make out a faint green glow in the distance, getting lighter the closer they got. Eventually the tunnel opened up into a large cavernous space. They stood at the top of a set of stairs and below them was the most amazing sight she'd ever seen. What looked like a million mythical creatures were gathered on a platform below them. Magical commuters waiting for a train that would never come.

Small flying beasts that reminded Lewis of large dragonflies, circled in the air. A creature with the body of a lion, a tail that looked like a snake and the hind legs of a goat, sat on the edge of the platform quietly licking its paws. A large horse with the torso and head of a man weaved its way in and out of the crowd, while a human shaped creature made up entirely of water played cards with a woman whose hair was full of snakes. Beings that looked to Lewis like dwarves were arguing amongst themselves, while two men with no heads but faces in the middle of their chests were sharing a bottle of whiskey.

At the far end of the platform a dog with two heads sat resting on its paws next to small, dirty looking man desperately scribbling into a ragged black book.

"I've walked into Narnia," Charlie gasped.

"No this is definitely Victoria Station."

"What are they all doing down there?"

"Trading, sharing, meeting, getting drunk together. This is one of the few places magical creatures can meet in the open so to speak and its neutral. No fighting here. Think of it like a watering hole. You know those you see on the tele. All kinds of creatures go there to drink. Lions drink next to Zebra and that kind of thing. They're more interested in spending time with mates than fighting. Everyone's safe down here. Well everyone that's magical that is."

"You said we need to keep our wits about us. Why if it's safe?"

"That's the thing, you aren't magical yet. Not fully anyway, so you don't count."

"You mean they can fight us?"

"Yes," Bob replied with a smile.

"Oh great," Charlie said with a groan.

"It's OK, you'll be fine as long as you stick with me, I promise."

"Somehow I'm not reassured."

"It'll be fine. We go for a walk and we have a chat with The Gatherer. Nothing to it."

"Except we need to be alert, stick with you and use the grains if anything happens. That doesn't sound too safe."

Bob smiled, shrugged and started to make his way down the stairs.

"I really don't like that guy," Charlie grumbled.

They quickly became enclosed in a press of magical beings as they made their way along the platform. Close up they were more amazing that ever. Each one seemed to shimmer in the green glow resonating from the platform's walls.

Bob carefully weaved a path through them, even stopping to have a quick chat with a creature that looked like a man, with the head of a goat.

"That guy has a goat's head," Charlie whispered.

"Colin's fine, but don't play him at cards, he's a real shark."

"Bob!" I gruff voice barked at them from behind a small tree with a face set in the middle of its trunk.

"Hi Gral, long time no see."

"Cut the pleasantries Bob, you owe me money," a small green coloured creature said, as it appeared from behind a branch. "Me and Des here are short 10 large and you owe us."

"Yeah, I know but you said I had a month to get you that money."

"That was two months ago."

"Well I've been busy, Blaine business."

"Not interested. Pay up wolf boy."

"I don't have that kind of money on me, I'll get it to you though. My word on it."

"You word's not worth much. You know the score, get me the money or I take it out of your legs."

"I'll get you the money, just give me a week."

The creature looked at him through jet black eye, its tongue darting in and out of its mouth.

"I'll give you your week but you owe me 20 large now."

"What!"

"20 Bob, call it a late payment penalty. This time next week or its your legs. Do you understand?"

"I'll get you your money."

"You better or you'll never get a game anywhere again. Not one you have to walk to anyway."

"What was that?" Charlie asked after Gral disappeared.

"Just a disagreement about money, nothing really."

"It didn't sound like nothing."

"Yeah well, let's get moving, we're drawing attention."

They reached the other end of the platform without further incident and stopped in front of the man and the two-headed dog. Bob waited for a few seconds then coughed politely.

"What do you want?" the man spat, without looking up from his scribblings.

"I have an audience."

The man paused and looked up. "It isn't in the book."

"It won't be."

"It has to be in the book, or you're not coming in."

"Like I said, it won't be, I've been sent by Blaine."

The dirty man sighed and shook his head.

"They all say that, what makes you different?"

"This," Bob replied, handing him a small fob watch on an elegant silver chain. The man took it quickly, his eyes greedily scanning its surface.

"Very nice, clearly an item from the shop. You sure you didn't steal it?"

Bob growled in reply.

"Just checking. If Blaine wants you to meet The Gatherer, then meet him you shall. You still need gold," he said, holding out his dirty palm. Bob dropped a gold coin into it, which quickly disappeared into the folds of the man's dirty clothes.

"Let them past," he said to the two-headed dog, which lifted itself off the floor with a whine.

The light from the platform quickly faded as they entered a large cavern, full of rubbish. Piles of rags, old

bicycles, prams, newspapers, cardboard boxes, rotting ted-
dy bears, plastic bottles, televisions, mattresses, crates, tires,
plastic bags and shoes filled the space. There was even a
cooker and what looked like a deflated bouncy castle. The
whole space stunk of rotting food and decaying flesh. Lewis
gagged as he walked in, quickly covering his nose against
the stink.

"What is that smell?" Charlie gagged.

"Shhh."

In a small clearing in the middle of the floor was dirt-
iest man Lewis had ever seen. He wasn't even sure he was
a man at first. His face was covered in matted hair that
hung in greasy lumps across his face. His ripped and dirty
clothes hung off him like bin bags and a stink radiated
around him like heat.

Cold, piercing blue eyes, staring out behind the hair,
were the only things that gave away his humanity.

Bob walked slowly towards him and nodded his head
in respect. At first the man didn't acknowledge his presence, staring coldly in turn at each person in front of him.
Then he cleared his throat, gathering a great glob of snot
in his mouth and spitting it out onto the floor in front of
him.

"Charming," Charlie murmured.

"You want to know where he is?" a gravelly voice
rasped from behind the curtain of hair.

"We're hoping you'd be able to tell us."

"Perhaps. I wish to speak to them first. Come forward, Lewis of the royal blood."

Lewis stepped forward tentatively. Trying his best to
breathe through his nose and ignore the stink surrounding
him.

"I see it in you, can you not feel it?" the tramp asked
after another long stare.

"Yes, I can feel it."

"Yes, but it is deep down child. Deep in your core.
You must work to bring it up. You must focus on your

power. Channel it, direct it until it is yours to command. Tell me, do you wish to kill Blaine or The Dark Man?"

"What?" Lewis asked, stunned.

"You have the power for either, I can see it there. It is your choice. A force for light or dark. Either path is open to you. You simply have to take the first step."

"I don't want to kill anyone."

"That path is not open to you. Kill or be killed, there is no other way."

"I want to protect my Mum."

"Then I will deem that the path of light. But be careful, it is easy to step either way. They will not tell you this. Those agents who only want you to do their bidding. Remember no one gives anything away for free. Every gift has a cost. It is why I take gold before we speak. So you know my fee. You already know The Dark Man's cost, but tell me what is Blaine after?"

"He wants to protect us," Lewis replied with a conviction he did not feel.

"Yes, I can see how it can look like that. Very well Lewis of the royal blood, go in peace. Charlie of the royal blood step forward."

Charlie stepped forward, tossing her hair away from her face and crossing he arms defiantly.

"Just so you know, I don't trust Blaine and I don't trust you either."

The tramp barked out a series of harsh laughs and shook his head.

"Then you are indeed a prophet amongst us. You do well to trust yourself. But I feel you can trust your brother of the blood too. You will not have to struggle to gain your power. It is there just below the surface. All you need to do is reach out and take it. But I feel you have to believe first. Strange considering all you've seen. It is yourself you do not believe in I think. Such a shame when you understand others so well."

"Yeah well I've had a hard couple of days and I could kill for a manicure."

"You will go far my daughter, far indeed," he replied smiling, showing a set of perfect white teeth. "Step forward soldier and hear me."

Bob stepped forward and listened as The Gatherer whispered to him.

"That guy's the weirdest we've seen so far."

"Totally, and the stink. I think I'm going to throw up."

"Do you think they'll mind if we go outside? I need cleaner air."

"No, they're gabbing away, let's get out of this place."

They walked out of the cavern and drew in breaths of cleaner air.

"What a stink," Charlie gagged.

"It is the smell of truth," said the ragged man sitting cross-legged at the entrance, never taking is eyes off his little black book.

"It's the smell of a guy in desperate need of a bath," Charlie replied.

"This is getting weirder by the minute," Lewis said. "Next we'll be meeting a wizard and a witch."

"Yeah, she'll ride in on a broomstick," Charlie said, laughing.

"Hooomaaan!" a booming voice said.

Charlie swung around and adopted a defensive pose without thinking. Lewis crouched down quickly and to his surprise began to growl. The atmosphere in the sunken station quickly cooled. The general chatter ceased and all eyes, faces and bodies turned towards Lewis and Charlie.

"I think we might be in trouble," Charlie hissed.

"Hoooomaaan!" the voice boomed out once again.

Magical creatures of all types began to shift as the biggest man Lewis had ever seen revealed himself.

"I don't remember seeing him when we walked in."

A creature Lewis could only describe as a giant, strode towards them. His massive arms and legs were bulging with muscles, while his chest seemed to go on forever. Dressed in a ragged blue toga and ancient looking sandals his body was topped by a tiny head, covered in bright red hair. A set of piercing blue eyes stared menacingly at them.

"Hooomans not here, this for magic, not you!" he boomed. The creature took a menacing step forward, stomping down a massive foot that sent shockwaves through the concrete floor.

Without thinking Charlie drew herself up and gathered her strength. The air seemed to shimmer around her then swirl and churn before drawing into her. For a moment she stood there motionless, a vortex of power swirling below the surface of her skin. Then she stepped forward and sighed. A blast of power exploded out of her, hitting the giant full in the chest and sending him reeling backwards. He smashed into the crowd of creatures like a bowling ball smashing into pins. Arms and legs, branches and fur, were sent in all directions, followed by a cacophony of screams and howls of pain.

Charlie drew herself up and smiled. "That got him."

"I think you might have been a bit heavy with that one," Lewis said, stepping backwards.

A multitude of magical creatures quickly dusted themselves off and turned towards Charlie with anger in their eyes.

"I was just defending myself. With magic too, I'm a magician," she said, stepping backwards towards.

"You're a human girl and you should not be here," a dwarf said with a squeaky voice.

"You used magic in here, you're not supposed to use magic, you broke the law," a water nymph said wetly.

"You're an abomination!" a man-shaped lizard hissed.

The mood of the crowd turned ugly as they shuffled towards Lewis and Charlie.

"Hang on," Lewis shouted, but his words were lost in the noise of general grumbling that grew louder as the crowd got nearer.

"They have to pay, they used magic."

"They are human, humans are not allowed here, they should be chucked out."

"They attacked us, they are just like all the rest, they're evil."

"They need to be taught a lesson."

"They need to die!"

Lewis and Charlie shuffled back towards the cave entrance as the mob grew closer.

"What do we do?" Charlie said.

"We defend ourselves, there's nothing else for it, get ready."

They both prepared to defend themselves. Lewis began to look inwards and feel the rush of power as it surged inside him. Its reassuring presence gave him courage. He was sure he could repel the first attack and he knew Charlie would be standing by his side.

"Hoooomans!" a voice boomed out across the platform.

The crowd instantly grew silent and all eyes turned towards the voice. Back in the middle of the crowd Lewis could make out the furious face of the giant Charlie had pushed away.

"Hooomans attack Gregor, Gregor now kill hoomans."

"I thought I'd dealt with that guy."

Gregor used his massive forearms to pushed magical creatures out of his way as he waded through the crowd. His face was now the colour of his hair and there was a murderous look in his eyes.

"Gregor fight hoomans and kill them."

Lewis planted his feet firmly on the ground and readied himself for the fight. The power churned inside him like a whirlwind. He wasn't sure how long he could keep it there and a part of him willed the giant to hurry up. He took in a deep breath as the creature reached the edge of the crowd and burst through. He could feel the power straining inside, willing to be released. He let his breath out slowly and pointed his arms towards the giant. A split second before he released his blood power, a snarling mass of fur and teeth rushed past him and hit the giant squarely in the chest.

Lewis jumped, screamed, and released his power into the mass just behind the giant. A horde of creatures was flung away from him, smashing into each other and skidding across the platform. Charlie released her power a second later, sending more creatures tumbling across the station.

Lewis staggered forward, feeling the last dregs of power drain out of him. His body shook with the strain of suddenly generating and releasing so much power. He wanted to curl up into a ball and sleep for a week, but he knew that wasn't possible. A multitude of creatures were picking themselves up off the floor. Each one of them staring at him with death in their eyes.

"Oh God," he whispered, taking another step back to the entrance to The Gatherer's cave.

"Come on," Charlie said, stepping in front of him and facing the horde head on. She could feel the power surge inside her. It wasn't coming from the center of her stomach as before, this time it seemed to flow through her veins and surge through her muscles. A feeling of invincibility permeated her being. She was ready to take on the horde in front of her, then go and find The Dark Man and his werewolves and beat them too. Nothing was going to stop her, especially not this pathetic group of creatures angrily making their way towards her.

Her skin began to sizzle and her muscles began to stretch as the change started to take hold. Charlie welcomed it with glee. Amazed that she had been afraid before. How could anyone be afraid of this much power?

She took another step towards the creatures and two things happened at once. The thing called Gregor, smashed his way through the crowd with Bob on his back. He staggered from one foot to the other, desperately trying to release Bob's jaws, which were currently sunk deep into his shoulder. His great arms whirled around as he did and his hand smashed off the side of Charlie's head, sending her backwards and into the two-headed dog. At the same time a water nymph reached Lewis and sent him over the side of the platform with a blast of ice cold water. After that, all hell broke loose.

CINDY'S NOT COMING HOME

Derek sat in the middle of the floor, surrounded by his treasures, and cried. He wasn't sure why he was crying, or why he was sat on the floor, when there was a perfectly good couch on the other side of the room, but he was doing both just the same.

He missed Cindy, he was sure about that. He felt the guilt of leaving her press down on him like a yoke across his shoulders. Of course, he hadn't left her, he'd abandoned her. Leaving her wasn't quite the same thing, but Derek wasn't ready to admit that to himself just yet. He also felt guilty that she was dead and he had lived. That she was at the bottom of a lift shaft, twisted into impossible angles, while he sat on the floor of his house, crying onto his shirt.

He could still see her writhing about on the floor, a million neon creatures stinging her skin and stuffing themselves down her throat. He tried to reach out to her. At least he'd convinced himself that was what he'd done. He tried to grab her, to brush the creature off her, to clear her nose and her throat, to send the evil beasts skittering back into the oven. But he couldn't, and now she was dead. As dead as the cold, creature gently rolling around on his palm.

It looked like a large dragonfly to Derek. But then again etymology wasn't one of his specialties, so he couldn't be sure. It had a fat body with a long tail, sat on top of six spindly legs. A bulbous head finished in a sharp stinger and its eyes, now a black as night, had flashed angry orange and green hues when it was alive. That bit Derek remembered with a shudder. He must have grabbed the thing when he was fighting for his life, but he hadn't noticed it, grasped firmly in his hand, until he'd burst, gasping and crying, into his living room.

He rolled it gently across his palm, watching orange and red colours ripple gently across its body. It felt heavy in his hand, like it had much more weight than it should for an insect of its size.

"What are you?" he asked himself as he absently wiped snot and tears off his face.

"Where the hell did you come from and why did you attack me?"

The creature remained silent.

Derek sighed and looked around his cluttered living room. His treasures looked dull and cheap to him now. Once thought of as the most important finds of the century, they now appeared to be just what they were, a horde of useless junk.

Cindy had been golden. Cindy had been a true treasure, a real find. But like everything you own, you only realise its true value once it's gone.

Derek didn't hear the knocking at first. It took a while for the persistent tapping to finally get through his veil of sorrow and self-pity.

"Who on earth comes knocking at this time of night?" he mumbled as he made his way to the front door.

He opened the door a crack to see a small man with large round spectacles blinking at him through the drizzle.

"Well, aren't you going to let me in? It's bloody freezing out here."

"Oh, it's you," Derek said without enthusiasm, opening the door to let the little man in.

"Where the hell have you been? We had a meeting tonight, did you forget?"

"A meeting, really?" Derek said absently, leading the cold man into the living room.

"Yes, a meeting. Seeing as you're the chair I would have thought you'd remember. You've never missed one before. I told the rest of the group he's never missed a meeting since the beginning Derek hasn't. There must be something terribly wrong if he's missed a meeting. That's why I'm here. What's gone on Derek?" he asked, shaking off his coat and taking a seat.

Derek answered by wailing into his hands and slumping down onto the floor.

"Oh, my man, what on earth is the matter?"

"She's dead Jamie, she's dead," Derek wailed.

"Dead? Who's dead?"

"Cindy."

"What!" Jamie sighed, his eyes wide with shock. "What do you mean she's dead? Oh, my God Derek, what happened."

"She was attacked, she was attacked and killed."

"Who attacked her?"

"These!" Derek wailed, holding out his hand.

The little man blinked as he looked down. There was a moment of silence as he took in the sight of the creature lying in the middle of Derek's palm. He took off his powerful spectacles and rubbed at his red eyes. Shaking his head as he did.

"Where?" he asked eventually.

"At the biscuit factory. You know how I like it and it was our anniversary so we thought we'd go there as a special treat and… wait, what do you mean where? You don't seem surprised to see this thing."

"I've seen them before."

"You mean you know what these are?' Derek asked, reaching forward and grabbing a handful of Jaime's shirt. "What are they? They killed Cindy, they attacked me and then they killed her. What are they!" He was shouting now, sending anger and spit straight into Jaime's face.

His friend didn't flinch, face remaining an impassive mask.

"What do you know?" Derek asked again, shaking him for emphasis.

After a few seconds of silence, Jaime took hold of Derek's hands and squeezed them gently.

"Not much. I know they are deadly when disturbed. I know they always attack in hordes and I know they're magic."

"What on earth are you talking about?"

"They're magical creatures Derek."

"Don't talk rubbish. Wait a minute, you're mocking me, aren't you? You're making fun of my pain?"

"No, I would never do that. I loved Cindy, we all did. She was a very special girl. I'm telling you the truth. You better sit down. There's more."

Derek looked into the eyes of his friend and realized he was telling the truth. He slowly sat back onto the floor and nodded for Jaime to continue."

"The world isn't made up the way you think it is. Oh, there's sky and sea and earth and all that stuff. But there's more, so much more and it's all sitting there right under our nose. Magic is real." Derek coughed and started to shake his head. "Oh, I know what you're thinking. He's gone mad. I thought that too at first. But Mr. Blaine explained it all to me."

"Who?"

"Mr. Blaine. I'll get to him. I was out on a scavenge one night. The usual, me, Ted and Marco decided to go to that old abattoir, you know the one right next to the railway track?" Derek nodded. "Well, we were exploring the killing pens just off the main hall, when a thing jumped out at me. I didn't know what it was at first. It was small and green and had large eyes and wings. It floated in front of me, then it ruffled my hair and flew away. I was shocked I can tell you. I thought I'd gone mad. Maybe I'd took in too many of the old fumes of dead cattle or something. But it was real. A part of me just knew it was real."

"What did the others say?"

"Nothing, they didn't see it and I didn't tell them. They would have laughed and told me to stop drinking the Kool Aid. I kept it to myself. Going over it again and again in my mind until I'd convinced myself that it was just an illusion brought on by lack of sleep or something. I even went searching for it on my own. Going back to the abattoir and into other places too, but I never found it. That was when I ended up in the shop."

"The shop?"

"Yeah you might have heard of it, Hound's Emporium? The kids call it the shop of curious incidents. Urban myth and all that. But I like it. It has a load of old stuff in it and Mr. Blaine buys some of my items. Well he grabbed my arm as soon as I walked in this time and looked at me in a strange way. 'When did you see it?' he asked. I knew what he meant straight away and I told him what had happened. He took me in the back and gave me a cup of tea. Then he told me all about magic. Told me the thing I'd seen was a fully-grown nymph and it must have liked me if it ruffled my hair. Now I'd seen it he could tell me all about magical creatures and stuff. But he warned me not to tell anyone else. Said they wouldn't believe me and would probably lock me up in the nut house or something. So, I didn't tell anyone, not even you. And since then I've been searching for magical creatures as well as treasures. Found some too. One that looked like a tree and one that took my money when we played cards. Really annoyed about that one."

Jaime stopped and shrugged his shoulders to indicate he'd finished.

"Is that it?"

"Well yeah, that's everything."

"But there must be so much more. I mean magical creatures exist. But why and why can't everyone see them? Some can communicate too by what you're telling me."

"Yeah and rip you off at cards."

"Jaime this is amazing. It's the find of the millennium. Can't you see that? We could be rich and famous."

"No, we can't!" Jaime replied forcefully. 'That was the one warning from Mr. Blaine. I can only speak to people who have seen them, like you. If I ever tried to speak to anyone else I'll be in real danger."

"What do you mean?"

"I mean I'll be dead. That world has to be kept secret. That's it's gig. If you're lucky enough to find it like you and me, we have to keep it secret too."

"Well, we'll see about that. I need more answers, I need to know why they attacked me and Cindy. I need to know where they came from and what makes them magical. I need to know everything."

"How are you going to do that?"

"Simple, we're going shopping."

WHO IS MR. MONO?

Calder stood under the flickering street lamp and wondered about the strange life he led. He was halfway between two worlds. Neither a thing of magic nor a human in the strictest sense. His mum had been a Lycan but for some reason the blood power hadn't been passed down to her son. His dad had been a plain old human, working on the trains all his life. He resented the fact his dad was normal and had passed his normality onto his son. But for him, Calder would have been a Lycan by now, fighting the forces of darkness and leading the charge into the fray. He could imagine himself changing in mid-air. His hand turning into a claw before it pounded into a werewolf's head. He'd have been a great Lycan warrior, he was certain of that. A commander of soldiers. A great leader, worshipped by his men. A general with many victories under his belt. Mr. Blaine would have sought his council,

The Dark Man would have trembled at his name. Armies would have fallen beneath his feet. If he'd been given his blood power. If his dad hadn't been so human.

But he had been and Calder had inherited it from him. He was condemned to be normal. Without power our influence. Great men didn't seek his council. He was never going to lead a charge into the fray. He was never going to claim great victories and no songs were ever going to be sung about his feats of bravery. Calder sighed and looked up at the flickering street lamp. It was broken and no one cared. It summed up his life.

"You seem to be melancholy this evening Mr. Rouge."

It took all of Calder's willpower not to jump out of his skin. The pale skinned weirdo had snuck up on him again.

"Just the lovely sunset affecting my mood Mr. Mono, didn't you see it?"

"I have no time for sunsets."

"Oh, come now, you have to make time for sunsets. Everyone needs a beautiful sunset in their life."

"I have no need for such trivial things. I am at the service of The Dark Man. What are sunsets next to that?"

"True," Calder replied, swallowing. To say anything negative about The Dark Man, in Mono's presence, was to meet a gruesome death. He had witnessed it.

"I assume you have news?"

"Yes, I went to the address you gave me," Calder said slowly.

"And?" Mono asked, leaning in.

"Well, I waited for an age, hours and hours. I was really worried someone would see me hanging around and call the cops."

"Did they?"

"No, I was really careful, just like you warned me to be. I waited out of sight, but in a spot where I could see the front door. You don't realise just how busy an empty street can be until you hang around for a few hours. It was like Piccadilly Circus out there. Cars and old dears passing all the time. Not to mention the little kids making loads of noise "

"Get to the point," Mono said flatly.

"Well, I waited like I said and I was just about to give up, didn't want to blow my cover or anything, when a kid appeared from around the corner. There'd been loads of kids walking about while I was there but this one seemed to fit the description you gave me. I got out of my hiding place and walked up to him as casually as I could. I figured I would be able to tell if I just walked past him. And well I did." Calder shrugged and dug his hands into his pockets. He wanted to appear casual and prevent Mono from seeing how much they trembled.

Mono blinked and stepped back. This was the first-time Calder had seen the human machine look so confused.

"And what did you see?" he asked.

"Well that's just it. I'm not sure."

Calder was lifted off his feet before he could utter another word.

"I'm sure I made it clear the last time we met, what I would do to you and your family if you failed me on this mission."

"No, wait," Calder managed to gasp through his reddening face.

"Wait for what? You've already told me you're not sure what you saw. I was very clear the last time we met. I was, wasn't I Mr. Rouge?" Calder could only cough a response. "Yes, I thought I was. You needed to properly identify the boy or confirm it isn't him, a very simple task. Now I could simply kill you right now and find a more reliable servant, or I could kill your family, while you watch. Which one should it be I wonder?"

"Wait, I found him," Calder managed to whisper.

Mono let go and Calder collapsed onto the floor at his feet, drawing in great gulps of air.

"Why didn't you say that in the first place?"

It took a moment before Calder could reply. He considered reaching inside his pocket and taking out the blade that hid there. Opening up Mr. Mono's throat was a very appealing thought right about now. But his family would pay the price as soon as The Dark Man found out.

"I was about to when you grabbed me," he managed to reply. "I'm not totally sure you see. I think he had an aura but if he did then it was really faint. I guess he doesn't even know it and if that's the case I guess it's not your boy. I figured he would have felt his blood power by now and the other side would have reached out to him and all that, and he arrived alone and looked totally normal. That's why I wasn't sure. I wanted to make sure before I gave you info. Don't want to give you any rubbish advise and all that."

"I'm so glad you considered our requirements for once Mr. Rouge, but you need to be sure. We need to confirm it is the boy we seek before sending out our troops and we have little time. I made that clear the last time we met."

"Yeah well, I was only trying to be helpful."

"A human trait I think."

"Who are you Mr. Mono?" Calder asked, anger suddenly coursing through his body.

"You want my help but you don't. You keep making these strange comments about humans, but you look just the same as me as far as I can tell. Don't get me wrong it takes all sorts and I have no problem with werewolves and other magical creatures, I'm just a bit confused by you, that's all."

"I am a servant of the master, that is all you need to know. Do your job and your family will be safe. Fail me and they will reap the whirlwind."

"You know you keep threatening me and my family for no good reason. I'm here and I'm doing as you ask, so stop with all the threats." Calder was angry now and getting increasingly reckless. He was sick of the fact his family was in danger and there was little he could do about it. Little until he'd spoken to Mr. Blaine that is. But he was hardly going to tell Mono that little secret.

"Why is it you can see the boy's aura?" Mono asked, throwing Calder off balance.

"What?"

"Well you're a human but you can see auras, why is that?"

"Because my mum was a Lycan. I get it from her."

"But you can't change, can you? You're not a Lycan?"

"No," Calder replied sullenly.

"No, just as I thought. I on the other hand can do many things. I am not of this world. I am not bound by your rules. Remember that the next time you raise your voice to me Calder. I am in a forgiving mood today. I may not be tomorrow and here you are a weak human."

Calder nodded, an icy finger of fear running down his spine.

"Go back and check again. Be sure this time. We will meet again tomorrow night."

Mono turned and strode away without another word.

Calder let out a sigh of relief when he was out of sight. That had been close. His recklessness had nearly costs him. He couldn't let that happen again. He was annoyed things hadn't gone to plan. He'd not got what he needed, which meant he'd have to meet Mono again. But it was worth the risk. He was committed now. He'd lied to Mono for the first time. There was no going. If Blaine didn't come through he was finished and his family was too.

AFTER THE CEREMONY

Zander sat in misery, a lock of Lila's hair held in her hand. She'd participated in the ceremony along with her team. Each one weeping silently as Blaine released Lila's spirit and honoured her blood power.

The sight of Lila lying cold and dead in front of her had been one of the most painful things Zander had ever experienced. She was convinced her heart was going to burst and it took all her remaining strength to stand there next to her colleagues, when all she wanted to do was crawl into a ball and cry away the rest of her life.

Her heart felt heavy. Her bones felt like they were made of lead. Her head ached and her throat was swollen and sore from all the weeping she'd done.

Lila was gone. Blaine had completed the Lycan ceremony and sent her on. Zander had never felt so alone.

She went over the fight in her mind for the millionth time. Lila had been on the edge of the field, essentially out of harm's way. She was meant to keep any stray werewolves from escaping, a job they'd all done a million times before. She'd even joked that it was one step up from babysitting and a lycan of her skill and ability shouldn't be doing it. But Zander had insisted. Reminding her that it was a job everyone had to do, but secretly trying to keep her away from the fighting and as safe as possible. But her plan had backfired spectacularly and the love of her life was dead.

"Should have don't it myself," she said to the empty room. "Should have known she was going to get hurt."

"There's no way you could have known that my dear," Blaine said, appearing from nowhere. "We have many powers but the ability to see into the future isn't one of them. Lila was a soldier, she knew the dangers as much as anyone. Blaming yourself and trying to second guess her actions, does not become you. It insults her memory. She would not accept you moaning and wailing. She would expect you to be out their getting revenge."

"You don't understand, you've never loved anyone," Zander spat. She knew that was unfair but she didn't care. She was sick of people telling her how she should feel, especially someone like Blaine, who she was sure had never loved anyone in his life.

"You're right, I do not understand. How could I? No one felt for Lila the way you did. Your love burns bright, everyone can see that, even though you tried to hide it. But do not make the mistake of thinking you are the only one to have ever loved and lost. We who guard the gate have lost so much. You know the history, you know the sacrifices we all have made. Do not insult her memory, or that of all those who have gone before, by weeping and pulling out your hair. Be a soldier Zander. Go and do what you do best."

"What's that?"

"Killing werewolves."

"That won't bring her back?"

"No, but it will prevent others ending up like her. Besides, the war never stops. Every minute we hesitate is an advantage to The Dark Man. He is getting closer. I do not have to explain to you what will happen if he finds what he seeks."

"What's that to me now?"

"Lila gave her life for the cause and I know you would too. You are hurting now and lashing out, but I know there's a part of you understands the danger we are all in. You are the last line of defense. If you fall, we all fall. You have never failed us and you will not now."

She knew that Blaine was right. The Dark Man was on the move, preparing his army, getting ready to strike. Whatever pain Zander was feeling, would be as nothing if The Dark Man was victorious. Besides, she had a werewolf to find.

"So where do we start?"

"The Gatherer refused, once again, to tell Bob where The Dark Man is hiding. However we need to go back to the tunnels, we've lost Lewis."

"What!" Zander gasped. "How? What the hell happened?"

"Bob took them to the station and they got into a fight with a troll. The got separated. Bob managed to bring Charlie out but Lewis is still down there as far as we know."

"He's as stupid as he is incompetent. How could you entrust them to him?"

"You know why. They need to find their blood power. The only way to do that is to put them in harm's way. Say what you like about Bob, he's good at putting people in danger."

"Which is fine when it's soldiers who can look after themselves." Zander moaned. "Well it's not fine but at least they have a chance. What chance does a couple of kids have?"

"We had no other choice, we are out of time you know that."

"You should have told them the truth and let them decide for themselves. Instead you spin them a yarn about a bloody key."

"We have done what we feel is best."

"Yeah, how's that working out for you?"

There was silence between them and Zander realized she was standing with her fists clenched. She took in a deep breath and sat back down.

"OK, I'll go and get him. But I take over when I find him. Bob can go back to bating werewolves for a living."

Blaine nodded, smiling inside. Zander could always be relied upon to rise to the challenge.

"Charlie wants to go with you, she's anxious to find Lewis."

"I'll move faster without her. Besides, she's been in enough danger for one day."

"She'll not rest until he's found, and I can't stop her going out to find him if she wants to."

Zander looked at him through stern eyes and shook her head.

"Are you that desperate for them to gain their powers?"

"You know we have no choice. Either we help them or The Dark Man takes them. They have a chance when their powers are developed. We all do."

"Yeah and I suppose it helps if you have all that power on your side."

"What would you rather have, me supporting them, or The Dark Man taking them?"

"Sometimes I'm not really sure there's a difference."

SLAUGHTERHOUSE 4

The warehouse smelt even though it was empty. It smelt of dead cattle and of horror and pain. Dark brown stains filled the floor and some bright spark had written 'Slaughterhouse 4' on a wall, in what looked like blood. Charlie hoped it was cattle blood or she was going to puke.

They'd set off as soon as Blaine had spoken to Zander. Charlie liked Zander, she was no nonsense. Focussed on the task at hand and clearly didn't like small talk. A real contrast from Bob and his casual way of getting everyone into trouble. For the first time in an age Charlie felt safe, even though they were going back out into danger. She could feel Zander's power and confidence radiate from her. They were coming off her in waves that warmed Charlie to her toes. She knew this was one of the reasons why she was no longer afraid, but it wasn't the only one.

Charlie was close to unleashing her blood power. It churned under the surface of her skin, ready to blast out at any moment. She was sure it would have been released at the station if she hadn't been knocked out. Her skin felt tight and thin. Her head pounded with the concentration it took to hold it all back and talking was difficult, another reason why she was glad Zander didn't like small talk.

Her legs felt heavy, like she was constantly wading through water, and her eyes kept going in and out of focus. She didn't know what was going to happen but she did know it was going to happen today. Probably amongst the smells and stains of the slaughterhouse. All of a sudden it felt silly that they'd been looking for a key. Charlie was sure she wouldn't need it to unleash her power.

"You OK?"

"What?"

"You don't look right. We can go back to the shop if you want and you can get some rest."

"No, no it's fine. I'm just a bit tired, I'll be OK."

"Fine, but let me know if you need a rest."

"Yeah sure. Why have we come here? Lewis disappeared in that underground station." Charlie asked, quickly changing the subject.

"I know, but there's an entrance to it here. I figure he might come out this way."

"How long has this place been closed?"

"I don't know. I think it's been closed for some time, why?"

"It stinks."

"Well it would," Zander replied, laughing. "It was a slaughterhouse. You can't really kill animals without making a mess."

"Yeah but the smell. I mean it's like they were killing here yesterday."

"You're right," Zander replied, her skin starting to tingle. "I think we best move on."

The wall exploded, sending plaster and bricks flying outwards. Zander instinctively reached across and pulled Charlie down, changing form as she did.

Charlie gasped as the hurricane blasted around her. It took her breath and pressed her flat onto the floor. For a second she was disorientated and briefly wondered why a dog was sitting on top of her. Then the sound hit her like a hammer, rattling her teeth and flapping her eyelids. She instinctively put her hands over her face and screamed as loud as she could. Plaster, brick and dust, raced across her body, stinging her skin, bouncing off her arms and legs and rattling through her hair. For a moment she was convinced the cloud of debris would carry her away, so powerful was the force around her. Then the dust settled and bits of plaster and brick stopped racing across the floor.

In a heatbeat everything was quiet. The dust settled around Charlie like a shroud. Coating her in a white layer of grime. She lay where she was and tried to focus on her breathing. She wasn't sure if she'd been injured in the blast and wasn't too keen to find out. After a few seconds of peace, she became aware of a ringing in her ears. A sound that started quietly but rose quickly into a clanging in the centre of her skull, making her teeth sing like a tuning fork and her temples thump along in sympathy.

She sat up painfully and took in a wheezing breath, immediately regretting it as she coughed up great globs of white spit. Her whole body shook with the effort of clearing her lungs. Her throat felt raw and her eyes streamed. Once she could breathe without coughing, she became aware of two things. Her skin had started to sing once again. An insistent chant, urging her to let go, to let the blood power take over, to let it flow through her veins. The second was the constant growling of a group of werewolves. By the sound of them, they were close.

Charlie felt anger bubble in the pit of her stomach. Quickly turning into a ball of rage that swelled and grew, making the very act of breathing painful. She stood up, an avalanche of dust and plaster tumbling from her as she did and took a staggering step forward. Her skin had become taunt across her body, pulling at her eyes and mouth, making it harder to breath and raising her fingernails from their beds. She could feel the seams of her skin start to split with the pressure. Her bones ached, her ears popped and her teeth began to stretch in her mouth. The ringing in her ears raised to the pitch of a howl and the hurricane of fury churned in her gut. Her body longed to let go, to throw out her anger, to get some kind of relief. She took another step forward and screamed at the top of her lungs. The blood power surged out of her.

The four werewolves advancing on her stopped in their tracks, The power blasting from her, washing over them like a tidal wave.

Every atom in Charlie's body seemed to scream at once. Her very existence fractured, then shattered into a billion pieces. Blasting out beyond the warehouse and up into the sky. She was aware of the slaughterhouse, the street outside, the city buzzing around her, the sky, the earth, and the millions of souls now held in the palm of her hand. She could hear the grass grow and the rats fight each other in the sewers. She could smell the rich odour of chips as a boy ate his way through a bag, sitting on an underground train. She could feel the anger of a mother berating her child for disappearing amongst the stalls in a market on the edge of town. She could hear the horn of a ship coming into port 50 miles away and the happy sound of children playing a football game in the next town along. The sound and movement of millions of lives vibrated through her. Each one was as familiar as her own face. She loved them and hated them in equal measure. Wishing them harm and wanting to protect them all at once. Babies cried, dogs howled, parents argued, children laughed and werewolves growled. The whole world was hers, all she needed to do was reach out and take it. The power was immense. No words could do it justice. She was the master of the universe. She could feel the wind brush a petal and gravity turn worlds all at the same time. She could change either with a thought. Her mortal worries were as nothing compared to the universe she now saw.

She glanced downwards, expecting to see rivers, oceans, mountains and valleys. Instead she saw a paw. It was covered in light brown hair and ended in sharp, white claws. The paw was attached to a leg. This was attached to a thigh, both covered in the same brown fur. The thigh was attached to a torso and right next to it was a dark brown hand with long fingers and wicked claws. This was dangling limply in mid-air. The torso disappeared from sight, up and below her eyesight.

Confused, she looked around and saw a large white room, the floor covered in a patchwork of rust coloured stains, white powder and rubble. It was a room smelling of fear and despair.

It was a small voice that told her the truth. It wasn't the booming voice of a God or the massive howl of a beast. It was quiet and frightened. It whispered to her from the middle of her mind. It told her one simple thing. 'Charlie, you're a monster.'

Charlie howled at the top of her enormous lungs, as the world came crashing in at lightspeed. Images of children, parents, rivers, streets, mountains and oceans all rushed away. She became small again. A tiny creature howling at the moon.

She was Charlie, she was a girl. She was Charlie, she was a Lycan.

The werewolves surrounded her, snarling and biting at the air. The smell of power radiating from her, the only thing that kept them from attacking on mass.

Charlie looked at them as if they were puppies. She knew that she could destroy them with a swipe of her hand. The thought terrified and amazed her in equal measure.

After a few more moments of snapping and snarling, the largest werewolf charged. With lightning speed Charlie grabbed its neck and snapped it. The sound ricocheting across the empty warehouse like a gun shot. It stopped the other werewolves as they were about to attack.

Charlie threw aside the corpse and charged. The fight didn't last more than a minute and would have been quicker if one of the werewolves hadn't tried to escape. When it was done, Charlie stood in the middle of the carnage and howled her delight.

The metallic smell of blood was strong in her nostrils, alongside that of dissipating fear and panic.

"Charlie," a voice said from the edge of the warehouse said.

Charlie the Lycan turned towards it quickly, a menacing growl escaping from her muzzle.

"You know me Charlie. It's Zander. I'm a friend. We came here together, remember?"

Charlie replied with a bark and a growl.

"We came to find Lewis, you remember Lewis?"

Charlie stopped in her tracks. One second she was readying to attack the strange weak creature on the other side of the room, the next she was trying to make sense of the name she'd just heard.

She knew a Lewis. But who was he and how did she know him? An image of a boy with light brown hair and ice blue eyes came to her. He was her friend, he was her companion. She'd saved him, she loved him.

The creature howled in confusion and rage. It wanted to attack. It could smell the aroma of fresh blood gushing around a weak body. But a growing part of it knew that it was wrong. Zander was a friend, Zander would take her to Lewis. Images of fighting and friendship clashed in her brain. She wanted to do both but she could pick only one. The new feelings hurt her, they were alien to a creature that sought only to hunt and kill. Charlie shook her great head and howled once more. The boy with the bright blue eyes just wouldn't go away.

She felt the change come quickly. The pain was excruciating at first. Her bones and skin contracted. The hair on her body withdrew. Her teeth shrunk and her nose reset itself. She writhed on the floor as a howl became a scream and then a garbled whimper.

Zander was at her side instantly. Covering her shivering body with a coat and helping her off the floor.

"It's OK Charlie, its fine. You're going to be OK."

Charlie shook in fear and loathing as the enormity of what she'd just done washed over her. She'd changed, she'd become a monster and the monster had killed.

"It's always worse the first time, but it'll get easier, I promise."

Charlie could only look at her through shaking strands of hair. She was afraid she'd vomit if she opened her mouth.

ON THE EDGE OF THE UNIVERSE

Lewis was wet. His clothes clung to him like a second skin, making every movement feel tight and heavy. He'd woken in the dark to the sound of rats and the smell of rubbish. Every part of his body ached and he'd taken an age to make sure nothing was broken. Once he was sure he could walk without doing himself damaged, he'd set off slowly. Feeling his way along the side of the tunnel, desperate to find light and fresh air.

Every sound was a werewolf waiting to attack. Every smell was a deadly toxin hurrying into his brain. He tried to tell himself he was being silly, but the dark and the damp made it hard to think straight. He didn't even want to think about what he was wading through.

He wasn't sure how he'd gotten so deep into the sewers. One moment he was fighting a giant, the next he was stuck at the bottom of the filthiest place on earth.

He'd scrambled around inside his pockets looking for the heavy grain of rice, but couldn't feel its reassuring presence. Finally resigning himself to the fact he was going to have to walk out of the sewer

He cursed Bob with every step. The idiot's recklessness had gotten them into trouble. They should never have gone into the station. But good old Bob didn't mind. He was happy to put them in danger, it was the best way to find the key after all.

He was sick with worry about Charlie too. She'd been about to change, he could see that. She needed help and support not a fight with a giant.

Lewis had been so sure of what they were doing at the beginning. He'd accepted what Blaine had said. He could see it in himself. He was different, he'd always known that. The revelations on magic and Lycans wasn't that much of a surprise. Unlike Charlie, it made everything click for him. He still didn't understand why he couldn't change and it worried him that Charlie looked like she was going to get her blood power before he was. But he'd accepted that there was a plan and it would all work out. It had to, otherwise the world would cease to exist.

Scrambling around in the smelly dark had changed his outlook. He wasn't as sure now. He'd become lost so easily. Abandoned down a sewer with rats and God knew what else. He should be able to help himself. His blood power should be able to show him the way. He was royalty after all. But he'd quickly become just a scared and abandoned teenager, with no clue how to get himself out of the mess he was in. The world was about to end and there was nothing he could do about it. He cursed Bob once more.

His thoughts wandered to his mum while he was scrabbling about I the dark. He wondered again where she was. He missed her smile and her warm hands ruffling his hair. He longed to hear her voice shouting at him to get his lazy butt out of bed and her rolling eyes when he told her he'd forgotten to put the bin out, again. He'd give anything to be warm and snug in his bed, the smells of frying bacon wafting up from the kitchen. If he was honest with himself he'd give anything to know where she was right now. She'd know what to do to get him out of this mess.

He was so focussed on wallowing in his own misery he didn't hear the light tapping of claws on brick. Even if he did he would have thought it was the rats finally come to take him. He didn't hear the soft brush of fur against the tunnel walls or the gentle lapping of water as paws waded forward. He didn't even hear the low, rumbling, growl, or the little yelp of excitement when one of the creatures realised it had found its pray. It was the smell that finally alerted him to the fact he was being hunted. A sharp, acrid smell like spilt vinegar. Totally out of place amongst the aromas of decaying rubbish and raw sewage. The smell led to the sounds and the sounds led to fear. Without thinking Lewis lurched forward, blindly racing down the tunnel. With yelps and barks of excitement, the werewolves gave chase.

He bounded off the curved walls and stumbled into the water, expecting claws to take him at any moment. He could hear them close behind, splashing through the shallow water and scrambling over the brick walls.

This was it, he either changed or died. Despite the fear and a pounding heart he tried to look inside, to find the power sleeping within him. All he found was a racing heart rattling around his chest.

He stumbled once again and went down into the icy water, his hands sinking into the soft mush on the sewer floor.

The first werewolf was on him in seconds, pushing him down in its eagerness to attack. The momentum taking it over and past his prone body.

Lewis felt the water engulf him and bits of debris bang against his head and neck. In desperation he tried to lift himself up, but his hands slipped on the slimy bottom and he fell further in. This saved him for a second time, as the werewolf had turned and lunged at the spot where his head had emerged only seconds before. It snapped at thin air and fell over his body, bowling into the werewolves that had followed and sending them scattering across the tunnel.

Lewis emerged from the bottom of the sewer, into a chaos of dark fur and limbs. Spluttering and desperately gasping in stale air, he lunged forward and began to wade quickly through the shallow water, desperate to get away from his pursuers.

The tangle of werewolves howled in fury as their prey ran away down the tunnel. They disentangled themselves in seconds and raced after him.

Lewis raced down the tunnel, bouncing off the curved walls once more as he splashed frantically through the shallow water. His heart raced at a million miles an hour, the hairs stood up across his body and his breathing came in rasping gasps. But despite all the terror coursing through his body he didn't change.

The lead werewolf closed the gap between them and slammed a massive paw into his back. It sent him flying forward down the tunnel and splashing into the dirty water at speed.

Anger course through him in that instant and without thinking he turned around and sent a powerful blast of energy smashing into the pursuing group of werewolves. They were sent racing backwards as the force of the blast hit them full on. He heard the snapping of bones accompany the sounds of pain and fear as the brown mass fell backwards. He was stunned by the strength of the force he'd sent at them and stood for a moment, staring with his mouth wide open. He'd created something strong enough to fell a group of werewolves. He forgot his fear as amazement and pride took over. That lasted until the first set of piercing red eyes emerged from the brown mess. That was enough to get his legs moving again and make him turn around and raced down the tunnel.

The werewolves were quick to followed, snarling and barking in fury at the blast that had taken them by surprise.

A sudden shaft of light illuminated an intersection. Lewis turned sharp right and picked up speed as he saw columns of light trail down the sewer in front of him. He must be getting close to the surface if light was spilling into the tunnels.

Running at full pelt, he scrambled down the tunnel, the werewolves following close behind.

Without thinking he stopped suddenly and sent another blast of energy into the pack. It wasn't as strong as the first, but it was enough to stop them and send some to the floor once again.

Without stopping to see if he'd broken any more bones, he continued down the tunnel. He now knew he had moments to work out an escape route before the monsters were on him. They'd be ready for another blast of energy and he wasn't sure he had enough strength to send another one at them.

The tunnel opened up onto a large space with a vaulted ceiling. A thick beam of light streamed down from the centre of the roof, Illuminating a circular patch of cartons, empty packets and condom, floating across the top of the dark water. Green lichen clung to the damp walls and graffiti proudly proclaimed 'Dez luvs Shaz' in large red letters along one wall, on another the words 'They are One', were written in a tall shaky hand. In front of him a number of tunnels were, interspersed at intervals along the opposite side of the room, each one leading away into the darkness.

This was his chance. If he could disappear down one before the chasing pack caught him, it would split them up and give him a better chance of surviving. If they followed each other down the wrong tunnel he might even get away completely.

Lewis picked one at random and started towards it.

The growling stopped him in his tracks. It was coming from the darkness in front of him and sent a shiver down his spine. Two red eyes appeared in the darkness, quickly followed by a set of snarling teeth. A face emerged next, then a powerful body, it's limbs ending in wicked claws. The sounds of angry werewolves was coming from behind him too. He was trapped.

"Now's the chance,' he said to himself. "Change you idiot or you're going to die.'

But he felt nothing but dread. No tingling skin, no fizzing blood, no hairs standing on the back of his neck. All he could feel was fear slowly rising in the pit of his stomach.

The chasing pack slowly began to fan out behind him.

This was it, he was going to be eaten by a pack of werewolves. As if sensing his predicament, the werewolves took their time. Savouring the fear that was pulsing out of him in waves. Snapping and snarling at each other as they did. Giving Lewis the impression they were arguing over who got to take the first bite.

Tears began to well up in his eyes and his bottom lip started to tremble. He didn't deserve this, he was just a lost boy trying to find his way home. An abandoned child, lost in the sewers, crying for his mum. Why did he have to be the one with all the blood power they craved? Why couldn't he have been normal like everyone else? He wanted to hang out with friends and gobble junk food while watching the latest zombie movie. He wanted to be shouted at for using his Mum's expensive shampoo. He wanted to go fishing with Charlie and argue with her about last night's football game. But most of all he just wanted to go home. To experience the smells and warmth of his Mother's love, to feel safe once again. The thought of Charlie brought more tears to his eyes. She was going to have to do this all by herself now and he wasn't sure she was up to it. It was hard enough with the two of them. The Dark Man was going to win, the world was going to end. But Lewis wasn't going to see that anyway, so why should be care? They'd put him in harm's way, a helpless boy with no idea what he was doing. Why should he care if their plans fell about their feet? They deserved what they got, they deserved The Dark Man.

He tried to imagine his Mother's face as he closed his eyes and waited for them to attack. He could remember the colour of her hair and see the scattering of freckles that ran across her nose, but he couldn't remember the colour of her eyes or the shape of her mouth. She was smaller than him but he couldn't remember if she came up to his shoulder's or his chin. These gaps annoyed him, making him realise how long it had been since he'd seen her. Anger started to well up inside him, despite his fear and dread. It bubbled in the pit of his stomach and warmed his skin. He could feel power begin to grow inside him, and the werewolves could too. The pack leader readied itself for the kill, leaning back on its haunches and raising its claws. A growl growing from its chest. It was so focussed on its prey that it didn't see the hoof until it was too late. It smashed into the side of its head, sending it crumpling to the floor in a dead heap.

The pack of werewolves didn't see the danger until it was too late. A mass of brown and black descended on them like an avalanche. Devouring them in blades and hooves and teeth and hands. The werewolves never had a chance. Within minutes the fight was over and a tangle of dead bodies floated gently in a dark red pool.

Lewis had kept his eyes shut as the whirlwind surrounded him. His frustration had instantly turned to fear as the tsunami ranged. He'd crouched low, his hands over his head. Waiting for the first blow that never came.

"You can stand up now," a gentle voice said next to him.

He opened his eyes to see a different group surrounding him. The werewolves had been replaced by the strangest creatures Lewis had seen, and that was saying something after a visit to Victoria station. They appeared to be men, but their bottom halves were covered in fur. Each one had wiry black hair on top of their head, with small horns sticking out of either side.

"What the…" Lewis stuttered.

"You're safe now. We've been following this lot for quite some time. They shouldn't be down here, they are an abomination. But it is settled now."

"Thank you," was all Lewis could croak in reply.

" My name is Silas," the creature said, holding out his hand. Lewis shook it silently.

"We will take you to the surface Prince of the Blood. You should be able to make your way back to Blaine from there."

The thought of the surface and his sudden release from an agonising death finally unlocked Lewis's jaws.

"Thank you. I got lost and they must have tracked me while I was wondering around the sewers."

"They can smell you my Prince. You must be careful and only move around in the open with your guards."

"Guards?" Lewis asked, confused. "Oh you mean Bob, well, we got separated, otherwise I would never have gotten lost."

The creature simply nodded in response, then turned around and moved towards one of the entrances. After a few seconds Lewis followed. The rest of the creatures surrounding him protectively.

The moved along the dimly lit corridor in silence, Silas taking the lead. Lewis quickly became disorientated. Not knowing if they were heading towards the surface or deeper into the tunnels. After a while he could see an amber coloured light up ahead. His hope growing that this was finally the way out. But hope was quickly turned to wonder as he exited the tunnel and gazed, open mouthed, at the sights in front of him.

SAVIOUR

“They are held in a safe house on the outskirts of the city,” Blaine said. “It isn't very well guarded and we should have no trouble freeing them.”

“They're arrogant,” Calder replied. “They didn't think I'd be able to find out where they're held or do anything to free them. Well that's a mistake.”

“We will free them,” Blaine replied. “But not until you've completed your task. We need you to find out where The Dark Man is if we are ever going to be able to protect our clan. We can't do that if you're compromised.”

“But I need to get them,” Calder whined.

“No, they can't suspect anything. I don't want you anywhere near the place.”

“They're my family!” Calder growled.

"Yes and I am going to get them for you, as we agreed. You need to keep up your part of the deal. Keep Mono onside and find out where The Dark Man is. After that we will reunite you with your family."

"No I need you to free them now. They're in grave danger, every second they have them is a second too much."

"No, you need to focus on Mono and your part of the deal. We'll get to them as soon as you do."

"That's not what we agreed," Calder said angrily.

"You will see them after you have fulfilled your half of the deal," Blaine replied casually.

"You're no better than them. What happens if I fail to live up to my side of the bargain? Will you kill them?"

"I am not The Dark Man. No harm will come to them. I need you to focus, that's all."

"But you don't trust me do you? You want to keep them in danger for as long as possible. As an insurance that I'll behave, that I'll not double-cross you with the Dark Man."

"You can see it like that if you want. But we have a deal. Fulfil your end, that's all I ask."

Calder sat down with a sigh. He was just as trapped as before. All he'd done was to replace Mono with Blaine, some saviour he'd turned out to be.

"All right, but we're done as soon as I get you the information you need and you get my family out."

"Yes."

"I'm due to meet him again tonight."

"Good, tell him the boy is the blood prince, and that he is unprotected."

"I don't see how that's going to help me find out where his boss is hiding."

"You'll have to use that considerable charm of yours Calder. You can get it out of him if you try. I have faith in you."

"Oh yeah I can see that."

The street lamp was still flickering.

"I'd have thought someone would have seen to that by now," Calder mused.

"Yes you would have thought so," Mono replied.

"I heard you this time," Calder said with a laugh.

"You were meant to. Well what have you got for me?"

Calder turned to look into the cold eyes of the creature and tried not to baulk at what he saw. They were empty. Totally devoid of anything you could call life. Calder didn't know what or who the creature was but it terrified him to think of it standing over his wife and kids.

"I have news, but we need to talk first."

"Oh really," Mono replied, raising one eyebrow.

"Yeah. Well, how do I know you'll keep your end of the bargain. How do I know you'll free my family?"

"Do you doubt my integrity?"

"Yes," Calder replied flatly.

"Very wise. But here's your predicament. You don't know if I'll release your family. But there is one thing you can be certain of, I'll kill them if you don't do as we demand."

Calder swallow and shoved his shaking hands into his pockets.

"I need to know they're safe, it's a simply as that. You'll get nothing out of me if they've been harmed."

"I could make you tell me."

"You could try. But remember this, I've got nothing to lose. Harm my family and I won't tell you a damn thing. Hurt me and I'll keep quiet just to protect them."

Mono smiled grimly and reached into his pocket.

"I like you Calder, you have spirit."

He quickly dialled a number on the phone that had appeared in his hand, then held it out to Calder, who took it shakily.

At first he could only hear crackling, then a familiar voice said hello.

"Jean," Calder said, "Jean is that you?"

"Calder, oh Calder, it's me."

"Are you OK love, are you and the kids safe?"

"Yes, we're fine, but get us out of here, get us home."

"I'm trying my love, I'll have you out soon I promise, just keep strong and look after the kids. I'll be seeing you soon."

Mono whipped the phone out of his hand and pushed it back into his pocket.

"Now, what do you know?"

Calder licked his lips before replying. "It's definitely him. No doubt about it. I saw his aura up close. It wasn't like anything I'd seen before. It had many colours, all shimmering and changing around him. My God the power was amazing. But he has no idea. He's just a kid. He has no idea who he is."

"Excellent," Mono purred.

"Wait there's something else."

"What?"

"Lycans. Loads of them. They're all over the estate. They must be closing in on him too. I thought you had werewolves around there, haven't you seen them?"

"No, there's been nothing."

"Well you best move quick. He's alone for now and vulnerable, but it won't be long before they find him. Oh and there's one more thing."

"What?"

"There's two of them."

"Two?"

"Yeah, a girl. No doubt about it. Just as powerful. Looks like his friend or sister or something, they're together a lot."

Mono nodded in reply, his cold eyes staring into the distance. "So they have found each other," he said, half to himself.

"Are you going to tell him?"

"Of course, he is the master, he will want to act quickly."

"What's he like?"

Mono smiled darkly. "He is nothing you could ever imagine. He is the whole world, he is the whole universe."

"But he hasn't shown himself, why not? I mean we all want to see him, to see his power. Why deny us that? I don't understand."

"When the time is right, you will see. You will all see."

"I can't believe no one has seen him already. He's The Dark Man, the most powerful being on earth. There must be a million creatures swarming around him right now, all wanting to worship him."

"There is no one but his minions. He will not be detected this time. He is safe until he is ready to reveal himself."

"Oh I see, well, let's hope he reveals himself soon. Now what about my family?"

"They will be released once we have verified your information. We need to pay this boy and girl a visit."

"Wait, why can't they be released now?"

"All in good time Calder. I am pleased with what you have told me, but we will be cautious and make sure. Stay by the phone, I will let you know when your family have been released." With that Mono turned around and walked away.

Calder let out a sigh and walked in the opposite direction. He needed to get to Blaine as soon as possible. Mono had finally made a mistake. It was time for Blaine to free his family.

THE HANGOVER

Charlie felt terrible. Her teeth ached, her eyeballs ached, even her hair ached, although she wasn't sure it was possible for human hair to ache. Then again she wasn't human anymore. She sat in the backroom of the shop and groaned. She didn't mind the pain if she was being honest. It distracted her from thinking about what she'd done in the slaughterhouse. Every now and again images of fresh flowing blood and broken limbs seeped through and she gave a shudder.

"Wow that's a bad hangover you've got there," Zander said sympathetically, as she entered the back room.

"I'm not hungover, I've not had a drink, remember?"

"Nah it's what we call it when we change back. It's way worse the first time, but it gets better, I promise. Here drink this, it'll help," she said, handing Charlie a steaming cup.

"What is it?"

"Blended bacon and eggs,"

"What?"

"Only kidding, it's tea. It'll make you feel better," Zander replied with a chuckle.

"So, what do you remember?"

"What do you mean?"

"Most people don't remember much after the first time. Apart from the rush that is and the power. God the power is amazing."

"I remember everything," Charlie replied quietly.

"Everything?"

"Yep, right down to the last detail."

"That's really unusual. Are you OK?"

"No I'm not," she replied weakly. "I changed into a monster and then I kill other monsters." I don't feel OK at all."

"They were evil Charlie, don't feel sorry for them. They would have killed you if you hadn't defended yourself."

"Yeah I know, but that's not what's worrying me. I liked it. I mean I really liked it. What kind of monster am I?"

"You're not. You're a soldier. This is war, make no mistake about it. It's them or us. There's no moral dilemmas here. No arbitration or peace talks. You can't negotiate with them, you can't make them understand. They're evil and they're controlled by pure evil. The only thing you can do is win."

"I enjoyed breaking their bones Zander. I enjoyed taking their lives."

"Let me tell you something. Those creatures have probably killed loads of humans, and just for the hell of it too. They don't hunt them to stay alive. They hunt them for the sport. That's evil and it needs wiping out."

"Don't we hunt foxes and stuff for sport?"

"It's not the same thing."

"Really, why not?"

"Because it's not. Foxes are just dumb animals and we hunt them to protect chickens and stuff."

"It seems the same to me. They're just dumb animals too, doing the bidding of their master."

"Well it isn't. You're going to have to get a grip. This won't be the last time you'll be in a fight and I can guarantee you that every fight from now on will be the fight of your life."

"You really know how to make a girl feel better," Charlie said with a smirk.

"Yeah I'm pure golden."

"After all that, we didn't even find Lewis."

"I thought it best if we just came back to the shop. You aren't in the right place for a rescue. We'll go out again tomorrow if he doesn't come back."

"We should go now. God knows what's happened to him."

"No, you need to rest. Besides, we've got others out looking for him and I bet they find him soon. Probably all snug and warm at home."

"That would be good," Charlie replied, suddenly more homesick then she'd ever felt.

"You know I think it would do me good to go home for a while. Get a good night's sleep and come back tomorrow all refreshed. It would be good to see my Gran."

"I don't think she's returned yet Charlie. Besides, it's too dangerous. They'll know where you live by now. You'll just be captured and given over to The Dark Man. Believe me, you don't want that."

"What do you mean my Gran's not there? I know I needed to be kept away from her while I'm finding the key. Well there's no need now. I've changed without it. I'm not a danger to her now. So why hasn't she returned?"

"You've only changed once. It takes a while to get to grips with it all. Give it a bit longer. When you can change without losing it, you'll be fine. As for your Gran, I don't know where she is. I think Blaine thought it best to keep her away from your house just in case some werewolves come visiting, I think that's why she's not come back yet."

"I see. But how long is it going to take for me to control myself? My Gran can come after that surely? I could protect her then."

"Not long, I promise."

Any further protestation by Charlie were cut short by the shouting that suddenly erupted from the shop beyond the curtain.

Charlie followed Zander through it and found a middle aged man, standing in the centre of the shop, sporting a beetroot coloured face and bulging eyes.

"I don't care what you say, they killed my girlfriend," he shouted in a shrill voice, full of righteous indignation. "They attacked me and they attacked her and I want them brought to account. I don't care how magical they're supposed to be, they need to be dealt with."

Blaine was stood next to him with hands spread out, trying to calm his fury.

"They are animals, it's as simple as that. You can't exterminate them all."

"I don't see why not."

"Because it would be cruel. They were protecting their territory. They would have seen you as a threat, that's why they attacked. These creatures read thoughts and moods. They attack when a thought feels dangerous. You must have been thinking about attacking them."

"I most certainly was not, and Cindy has never had a dangerous thought enter her head."

"That's very true, she was a really kind person," a short man said from behind his angry friend.

"Yes and she clearly loved you Derek, that's why they attacked her, she was defending you," Blaine replied.

"Everything OK Mr. Blaine?" Zander asked in her most official sounding voice.

"Everything's fine Zander, thank you. Derek here had an encounter with a swarm of Flitterbys."

"Nasty. It's mating season, they're especially aggressive right now. Best not to provoke them."

"Yes well that was something I wasn't aware of," Derek said gruffly, "and neither was my partner."

"I can see how that would be difficult," Blaine said soothingly. "I'm sorry for your lost. They are passive creatures, most of the time. But as my colleague has said, mating season is particularly difficult. They are sensitive to thoughts at that time."

"Is that it? Is that the best you can do? My girlfriend is dead because of them. What do we do about it?"

"Do? I'm sorry there's nothing we can do. You don't arrest a lion if it eats a zebra. This is the same."

"You shoot the lion that's what you do," Derek replied angrily. This wasn't going the way he had hoped at all. He thought this Blaine character would offer to help. Tell him all he knew of the magical creatures living in the city. Maybe even give him a guided tour. Show him all the magical nooks and crannies the city had to offer. Then he could go to the nearest newspaper and make a fortune. It would make him world famous he was sure. The indifference he was encountering just made him angry.

"We have to track them down and exterminate them. Then we have to make sure there are no more around the city."

"Flitterbys are one of the least dangerous creatures I know. We're not going to track them down any more than we are any other magical creature living. I'm not an exterminator, I'm a shop keeper."

"Well if you won't help me I'll go myself. Jaime's seen magical creatures too. Now we know what to look for we should find them easily. Then I'm going to take action. I think the police and the council will be interested in this."

Blaine sighed and slowly folded his hands. He stared quietly at Derek, then shook his head. "Very well. If you are determined to put yourself in danger there's nothing I can do. But I will protect the creatures. Come back tomorrow and I'll send you out with some of my colleagues. They can show you what to look for and how to avoid getting hurt. But know this, I will not allow you to harm a defenceless creature. A Werewolf or a Troll is one thing, but a Flitterby is quite another."

"Werewolf? What do you mean werewolf?" Derek asked, swallowing hard.

"For your sake I hope you never have to find out. Come back tomorrow. Alone. And say nothing to anyone. If you do, you'll get no help from me, understood?"

Derek nodded eagerly and gave Jaime a sly smile.

"Until tomorrow then." Derek said, leaving quickly before Blaine could change his mind.

"I don't think that was very wise do you?" Zander said.

"Oh he's a gold digger, you could see that. Using his girlfriend's unfortunate death as leverage. There's only one way to deal with people like Derek and that's to scare them senseless. Bob can take him out tomorrow and introduce him to a mountain troll or something. He'll fall over himself to get away."

"You know best I guess, but don't come running to me for help when Bob gets the guy killed."

"Yes well, I'm sure it won't come to that. How are you feeling Charlie?" Blaine asked, quickly changing the subject.

"Like death warmed up."

"Ah, yes, the hangover. Don't worry it won't last long, and it gets easier every time you change. The most important thing is that you have changed. You've released your blood power. My goodness I can feel it from here, it's quite intoxicating. We'll need to do something about that. I've put extra wards around the shop so you should be safe here but it'll be like a klaxon call to every magical creature within a 100 miles every time you go out if you don't learn to control it quickly."

"How do I do that?'

"With you mind. Zander will show you how. Don't worry it's not that difficult."

"Well we need to do it quickly, I need to go and find Lewis."

"Oh don't worry about that, he's been found."

"When?"

"I just got word before our friend Derek arrived. He's with the Satyrs."

"Oh good, that's a relief," Zander said, exhaling heavily.

"Is it? What are the Satyrs?"

"Friends Charlie. They saved him from a group of hunting werewolves. He'll be home first thing in the morning.

"Is he OK?" Charlie asked anxiously.

"Yes, he's quite safe. If I know the Satyrs, he'll be having the time of his life."

HAVING THE TIME OF YOUR LIFE

The werewolf smashed through the window and landed heavily in the back garden. It rose quickly, a cascade of broken glass falling from its body like water, and dived back into the house.

Sounds of breaking furniture, smashing plates and snapping bones emanated from the house like party tunes. Anyone walking past would have thought the party inside had reached a particularly lively stage and no doubt would have phoned the police. Luckily enough, Lewis's house was fairly isolated and no one walked by in the middle of the night.

The front door suddenly burst outward and rattled across the lawn. Coming to rest against a small bush. The sounds of fighting increased as they spilled out onto the front garden. Teeth and claws flashed in the cold moonlight as warm blood stained the frosty lawn.

Mr. Mono watched the enfolding carnage from his vantage point, with cold detachment. It was clear that his werewolves had walked into an ambush and that Rouge had betrayed him. He suspected they'd tried to rescue Calder's family while his attention had been on the boy's house. But no matter, he'd already had his revenge on him. He smiled as he realised Calder would soon experience the exquisite pain reserved for traitors. Regardless of this setback Mono promised himself he would find the boy and girl and make them a present to his master. He knew he now had to do this or face the consequences of failure. The Dark Man did not easily forgive those who failed him. For the first time, the creature experienced fear, although he didn't fully understand the feeling. He would have to come up with a way to get back in his good graces, quickly.

The boy had been here, he could smell the faint odour of blood power circulating the house. It smelt of a power Mono had never experienced before. The boy was clearly of the royal blood and would make a powerful enemy if allowed to live. Better still, once caught, he would feed The Dark Man and enable the portal to be opened for the first time in a millennia. The thought of hordes of demons ravaging across the earth made Mono salivate. He would finally be able to join his family and eat his fill of souls. He would gorge himself on fat, juicy humans. The ones he had seen here had grown lazy. They knew nothing of the magical world and even less about how to protect themselves from a demon attack. It would be like taking candy from a baby.

Once he had eaten his fill, he would stand at the right hand of The Dark Man and rule the earth, basking in his mighty shadow. He had earned his reward. He had been his master's loyal servant for over as long as he could remember. Remaining at his side through his many failed attempts to open the portal. It had been Blaine who had thwarted him all this time. But with the boy's power on their side, Blaine would be easily overcome, and the portal that lay protected under his pathetic shop would finally be opened.

He smelt the lingering odour one more time and caught a sweet smell of perfume. A beautiful face full of love suddenly flashed before his eyes. Mono couldn't really remember his past. He knew he had been human once. He knew he had loved and lost. He faintly remembered a wife and children, and imagined the beautiful face had been that of his long dead wife. But he was sure that was just a dream. The Dark Man had freed him from the mortal world. Making him a powerful demon, making him his servant for all eternity. What was love or loss compared to The Dark Man's power and the sweet taste of human flesh?

The painful howl of a werewolf in its final death throws brought him out of his reverie. The night was lost. It was time to leave and plan the next steps. He needed a plan that would capture royalty. If he didn't he was sure The Dark Man would make him pay.

Lewis sat back and belched. He'd just eaten the best meal of his life. Burgers and chips followed by chocolate cake and ice cream. After so long without a proper meal it'd felt like eating a banquet. His stomach complained about the amount of food it had to digest and he belched deeply once again in response.

"Sounds like you enjoyed that," Silas said, entering the room and sitting next to him.

"That was amazing, thanks."

"No problem."

Lewis took another look at his saviour and smiled.

"What's so funny?"

"Nothing. If you'd asked me a few weeks ago that I'd be talking to a Satyr after he'd saved me from a bunch of werewolves I'd have thought you'd gone mad."

"It must seem weird to you?"

"It does. Never mind that I had no idea what a Satyr was before I met you."

"I had no idea what a human was before I met you," Silas replied, laughing.

"Really?"

"Nah, of course I did. You're hard to miss, there are millions of you."

"So you all live here under the ground?"

"Yep, we call it the Sanctuary. My tribe has been here for generations. We once roamed the earth, then you lot came along and it got harder to survive while you were around so we came here."

"Really? Sorry about that I had no idea."

"Why would you? You didn't even know about magic until a few weeks ago. I bet we're not exactly a popular topic taught in your schools."

"No, not really. Although I think school would be way more interesting if you were."

"A war's been raging, between Lycans and Were-wolves for a millennia, and it's one of the reasons why magical creatures have gone underground. But it's not the only one. Your ancestors couldn't cope with magic. They rejected it and rejected us. We were hunted and killed by your kind. We had to go underground, or in hiding, to survive them as well as the werewolves. Since then you've managed to forget all about us. That's almost worse than being hunted."

Lewis could only shrug his shoulders in response.

"Don't worry, it's not your fault. And besides, you'll be one of us once you turn, so you can blame the humans as much as we do after that. So what do you think of the Sanctuary?".

"It's amazing, I just can't get my head around it."

The sight that had greeted Lewis on his arrival had been like nothing he'd ever seen. He suspected no human had. The Sanctuary was an enormous cavern, rising hundreds of feet into the air. The floor was covered in small wooden houses, lush green parks, and hills covered in purple heather. A large lake fed by an enormous waterfall was on one side, and beside it stood the largest tree Lewis has ever seen. It's branches seemed to disappear into the roof of the cavern. Spreading out from the massive brown trunk like welcoming hands. Bright yellow fireflies flitted in and out of its branches, while a large red and black snake gently curved its way up the trunk.

"What is that?" Lewis had asked with awe.

"That, is the source," Silas said with pride.

"The what?"

"The source. It's the most sacred place on earth. You me, Bob, are all children of the source. Without it we would be like sheep lost in a blizzard."

"So it's like some type of tree God or something?"

"No, it's no God. We are all inter-connected you see. All magical creatures. We are connected by the source."

"Even the evil ones?"

"There isn't really such things as good or evil. There is only existence and nothingness. The source binds it all together, keeps us on this planet, keeps the power in our souls."

Lewis shook his head. The idea of a large tree being the root of all magical life on earth was too hard from him to understand.

"What if the Dark Man knew about this place?'

"He does. The source isn't like blood power, you can't take anything from it. He has no reason to come here, he can't take the source or own it. He just has to let it be."

Lewis cocked his head to one side and concentrated on the sound he could hear coming from the direction of the tree.

"I can hear singing."

"That's the source. It talks to all living creatures. Most trees do. Haven't you heard it before?"

"Tree's talking? No that's not really a thing in Mount Vernon," he said, laughing.

"Trees talk all the time you're just not listening. They're particularly noisy when the wind blows."

"Yeah I hear that, but that's just the leaves rustling in the wind."

"No it's the trees talking to each other. They're just shouting so they can be heard over the wind."

"Whatever you say," Lewis replied shaking his head. If a tree could live underground and sing to anyone that got near it, then trees near his house could talk too. He would have to listen more carefully in future.

"This is all very strange."

"Yes, I can see it is hard to understand. Just know it is here and because of it so are you. The humans on the other hand are a different story. I'm sure they'd cut it down if they found it. Then we'd all be doomed."

Lewis thought about the large tree as he sat back and belched once more. It seemed that the Dark Man wasn't the only thing he needed to worry about. He had to worry about his own kind too. Silas was right. Most people wouldn't believe you if you told them about magic, or described all the amazing creatures living under the city. If they did, they would want to use them to make money. He was right about the tree too. Something like that would just end up as fire wood.

"I've just heard from Mr. Blaine," Silas said, bringing Lewis out of his reverie. "He says he's sending Bob to come and get you in the morning."

"Oh good. I'll be able to thank him properly for abandoning me in the tunnels."

"Bob is a special creature."

"Yeah, he is," Lewis replied laughing. "So I guess I'm staying here until he comes?"

"Yes, it's safe here. You could focus on your blood power while you're here. Being so close to the source may help."

"Is it that obvious?"

"That you have yet to unleash your powers? Yes. But every lycan is different, and I can sense it is just beneath the surface for you. It is very powerful. You just need to find the key to unlocking it."

"That's what we've been doing. We just can't find it."

"Can't find it? What do you mean?"

"The key. We've been searching for it."

"Is that what Blaine has told you to do?" Silas asked, shaking his head.

"Well yeah," Lewis replied defensively.

"The key isn't a thing. It certainly isn't an actual key. It's the term lycans use to describe the one thing that will unleash their blood power for the first time. It is different for everyone. You'll find it eventually, it just takes time."

"So Blaine was lying, why would he do that?"

"I don't think he was technically lying, he was being economical with the truth. If you were down in the station before turning there's only one reason. To put you in danger. Fear, anger, sadness, are strong emotions known to bring on the change. It sounds like Blaine was trying to accelerate the process."

"He could have just told me!" Lewis said. Angry at himself for believing Blaine and angry at the strange man for putting him in so much danger."

"Yes he could have. But Blaine follows his own path."

"Well it didn't work. I've been terrified for days and it hasn't made any difference."

"Then fear isn't the trigger. You'll have to think hard. Did you feel the power growing in you at any time?"

"When we practised pushing."

"Well yes, that would work, but it's only like kicking a bucket full of water, it won't make you change, it will only give you a sense of how full the bucket is. You need to find the one thing that will kick the bucket over."

Lewis thought of all the situations he'd found himself in over the past few days, but nothing came to mind.

"No matter, it will happen. I just hope it's soon. Blaine is right about one thing. We need you to change quickly, or the Dark Man will find you and then we're all doomed."

"Great, just what I needed, another motivational speech."

Silas laughed and clapped Lewis hard on the back.

"Get some sleep human, you're going to need it."

SOMETHING'S HAPPENING AT THE ZOO

It wasn't as much a zoo as a collection of empty cages and broken fences. The zoo itself had been closed for years, the animals long since moved on and the keepers sacked. What remained quickly fell victim to vandals and suspicious types. A large fire burnt through the visitor's centre, locals 'borrowed' the wooden fencing and more or less anything else they could use and squatters claimed the old reptile house. For years it was known as a blight in an otherwise pretty area. Locals told their kids to avoid it, the council promised they would redevelop it, but never seemed to get around to starting. A Russian property developer even announced he would buy it and make it the greatest theme park in the west. He quickly disappeared in a cloud of scandal and suspicion.

So the place just sat there, getting more and more rotten. A dark heart at the centre of the city's soul.

The rumours of demons surfaced soon after the Russian disappeared. Just nonsense at first. Childish stories of beasts with red eyes and sharp fangs and a pervading smell of wet dog. Cats avoided the place and dog walkers started to take alternative routes that avoided going near the zoo. If you asked them they did that they would say that their dogs would start to whimper every time they got near to the entrance.

People got worried when an old tramp disappeared. He'd lived in the area for years, walking around with an old shopping trolley full of rubbish. One day he was there, the next he was gone. To be fair it did take folk a few weeks to realise the tramp was no longer around. The police conducted a half-hearted search and eventually found his body in a ditch, just outside the zoo. Rumours quickly spread that he was as stiff as a board and had a look of absolute terror on his grimy face, when they found him. People remembered the stories of beasts with red eyes and sharp fangs and put two and two together and surprisingly came up with four. But no one really believed that the tramp had been killed by a monster lurking in the old zoo. They just went about their everyday lives and avoided walking their dogs past the entrance.

Charlie took a deep breath and look over at the broken gates with the faded 'Welcome to Glasgow Zoo' sign above them.

"Are you sure we need to go in?"

"Yes, we have them by the short and curlies this time. The Dark Man's in there and if Calder's intel is correct, he's only guarded by a few werewolves," Zander replied.

"How sure are you about the intel?"

"It's solid. Obvious really, there's a load of Buckthorn trees at the zoo. It's great at masking the presence of blood power. He's been hiding there all along. I'm surprised Blaine didn't think of it. If Calder's rouse works, he'll have sent all his soldiers over to Lewis's house, and straight into a trap. That just leaves him and a few of his minions left."

"I hear this creature's really powerful."

"He's nothing compared to you, why do you think he's been hiding? He knows he's done for if Blaine got to you first, and that's what happened."

"OK, so I have to kill him."

"Yep."

"How?"

"How did you kill those werewolves in the slaughterhouse?"

"I don't want to think about that."

"With your power, it's as simple as that. There's never been anyone like you before. You're like their atom bomb or something. You can end this tonight. Finally we'll be free of these monsters."

Charlie swallow hard. She felt like a monster herself. Sometimes it was hard to separate the heroes from the bad guys.

They entered the zoo at pace. A group of lethal predators, silently searching for their prey. Zander and the rest quickly turned, but Charlie paused. She didn't want to feel the way she had before. It had been amazing and terrifying all at the same time. She was afraid that she'd never be able to change back. That the monster would consume her and she'd remain a snarling, hate-filled animal for the rest of her days.

The lead werewolf paused to look back at her. She knew it was Zander and she knew she was urging her to change. The rest stopped too. Now all of them were looking at her with expectant stares.

There was nothing else for it. She couldn't let them down. She swallowed hard and focussed all of her thoughts on the change. It happened easily this time, but the weird sensation of being out of herself was there, as was the awful pain of her bones snapping and repairing themselves.

The power was there too. An awesome sensation that made her feel she could do anything, kill anyone, break anything, change anything. And yet it felt more contained than the first time. Like it was tethered to her somehow. A power she could control, for good, or for ill. She shook her massive head and loped after the pack.

They spread out in groups of two and began searching the abandoned buildings and cages. The stench of dead bodies and dried blood was strong in Charlie's sensitive nostrils. There had been a lot of death here, the cages and floors reeked of it. It took all of her will power not to turn and flee. She ground her fangs and concentrated on keeping up with her companion. She knew she was hunting with Zander, but it was difficult to believe the amazing, silver-coloured creature in front of her was her friend. She smelt the same and her mannerisms were the same, despite her change, but one moment she'd been a confident soldier, the next an impressive looking lycan. It was going to take Charlie some time to get use to all this.

They entered the old chimp enclosure and spent time carefully inspecting the trees and rope walkways inside. The stench of fear and death was even stronger in here and for a time Charlie was sure she was going to be sick. She rubbed her nose on the ground in a desperate attempt to take the smell away. When she looked up, her heart sank.

Zander was standing in the middle of the enclosure, her body rigid, the hairs on her back and neck standing up. A low, threatening growl escaping her lips. In front of her stood three massive werewolves. Each one sported flaming red eyes and dripping fangs. Their hot breath sent the air in front of them white.

Charlie forgot all about the stench, and stepped slowly forward to stand next to Zander. The werewolves stepped back when they saw her, uncertain of how to deal with such power facing them down. Charlie smiled inside and stepped further forward. This was going to be easy, and this time she was in control. She would frighten them, maybe give them a knock or two, but she wouldn't need to destroy them as she'd done the last time. She could avoid being the monster she was terrified of becoming.

She began to channel her power, feeling the vortex churning inside her, making her fur sizzle and her blood boil. A ranging torrent of power, fighting to be released. It took all of her concentration to hold it back, all of her will to keep it in check. She knew she'd be able to level the entire zoo with one howl if she let it go now.

Zander and the werewolves could feel the power emanating off her like heat. They whined and clawed at the earth.

Charlie was aware of every blade of grass and flower petal living in the enclosure. She could taste the hot metal of old blood particles floating in the air and hear a worm burrowing under the damp earth. She could sense this all in an instant, but she missed the Dark Man's approach.

Just as she was about to release her power and knock down the enemy in front of her a new feeling suddenly engulf her. The cold black presence made her feel like she was being plunged into an ice bath. It damped down her power in an instant. Taking the breath from her and robbing the feeling from her limbs. She collapsed to the ground, a weak as a new born.

The Dark Man strode slowly into the enclosure, casually swinging a bright silver sword in his right hand. A cold fog whispered from his shoulders, clinging to his bright black hair and wrapping around his jet black morning coat. Charlie could see two red eyes staring at her from behind the black curtain of his hair.

She tried to get up, but her limbs wouldn't respond. She tried to channel the power inside her but her stomach felt as empty as a cold furnace.

"You cannot stand alone against me," the creature whispered. "Surly Blaine would have told you that? It was silly of you to come her alone Charlie. It is Charlie isn't it?" She could only manage a quiet whimper in reply.

"Yes I thought it was. Mono said you'd found each other. Blaine did well to protect you both for as long as he has, but he was reckless letting you come here alone. Do you really think your little ruse would work? Do you think I would let all my children leave me?"

The Dark Man raised his arms and a cohort or werewolves appeared around the sides of the enclosure. One or two of them held limp and lifeless bodies in their mouths. Clearly what remained of the lycans taking part in the raid. It had been a trap all along. He knew they would be coming to get him.

Charlie heard a whimper of pain coming from beside her and managed to move her head enough to see Zander writhing around on the floor.

"Yes, I knew all about your little plan. I can always count on Blaine to be obvious. And now what do we do with you?"

Zander let out a roar of anger and pain. Bounding up from the floor, she flew at the Dark Man, a bark of defiance bursting from her jaws. He simply stood where he was and waited for her to approach.

She leaped into the air the distance closed between them, her powerful front paws outstretched, the claws aimed at the Dark Man's throat.

At the last second he moved at impossible speed, letting Zander fly past him. He brought the blade down as she passed and severed her head from her body.

She'd turned back into a human before her head hit the ground. It bounded off a tree trunk and came to rest in the middle of an old tyre.

Charlie let out a howl of despair as she watched her friend die. This was not how it was supposed to be. She was all powerful. A royal princess with blood power flowing through her veins. And yet she'd been cowed by the Dark Man's power the instant she faced him.

"Do not weep for her Charlie," he whispered. "She had uses yet. As for you? Well we will have to find out the best way to eat you."

Charlie was sure she could hear him chuckle as he approached her, but thankfully she lost consciousness before he got too close.

BRING LOW THE SCHOOL

Midgy was hiding in a school cupboard and he was scared. He knew that because he was sweating. He always did when he was scared, It could be minus 10 but he'd still sweat buckets. Attending school at The Maggot made most of the pupils sweat. It's proper name was St Margaret's High, but only the head teacher called it that. This time it was the silence that made him so frightened. It seeped in under the bottom of the cupboard door like mist. Clinging to him, making him feel suffocated. He realised he was holding his breath and let it out slowly. Even so the noise sounded like he was screaming and he stopped half way through.

The cupboard smelt of pencil shavings and mouldy paper. A thin sliver of moonlight seeped in from a small window high up on one wall. It turned the shelves of books and jotters a strange silvery colour. If he squinted his eyes he could almost imagine they were hordes of bright treasure. If only there was a silver sword and shield on the shelf, but no matter how hard he screwed up his eyes, they would never appear.

The night had started just like any other. Midgy was a member of the Knight Shift, a band of pupils, who walked the halls of the school at night, looking for ghosts and ghouls. They thought of themselves like knights of old, protecting pupils from the horrors hidden in the darkest places. The Maggot was the darkest place of all.

Strange things happened in the school, it was a hotbed of evil. Strange creatures stalked the halls, evil smells emanated from classrooms and pupils went missing every now and again.

The adults dismissed it all as the wild imaginings of a few disturbed children, but the pupils knew better. The Maggot was alive and it wanted to eat your soul.

A group of the bravest, Midgy included, banded together and vowed to destroy the evil that lurked in dark corners. They became the Knight Shift, and now spent most of their evenings walking the halls and fighting whatever they found. The school wasn't alarmed and you could get in quite easily if you knew which window to open. They successfully battered away a ghoul or a strange tree shaped creature most nights.

During this particular night, everything was going well until the werewolves turned up. They were after blood, Midgy's and his friends in particular.

It started with the sounds of breaking chairs and smashing glass. When the Knight Shift went to investigate they stumbled upon a group of large dogs, rampaging in and out of classrooms. They turned on the small group of kids as soon as they saw them. Sticks and rolling pins were no match for teeth and claws. Midgy saw Ryan, one of his best friends go down first. Disappearing under a storm of snarling fangs. The rest fought bravely, even managing to get off a blow or two. But they turned and ran as soon as Gemma went down under the massive paw of a werewolf with silver fur and burning red eyes.

Midgy knew the halls well, and this saved him. He went downstairs instead of up. Giving him the chance of getting out. The werewolf chasing him snapped at his heels as he raced desperately down the hall. It bounced off the walls and smashed down the ceiling lights.

Midgy burst through a set of double doors and threw them back behind him. They clattered into the werewolf as it approached. This gave him the time he needed to scramble into a room with a large cupboard he knew was safe. You couldn't trust most cupboards in the Maggot.

Since then he'd stayed as still as he could, silently sweating buckets and wishing he had a sword to fight with.

It'd been quiet ever since he started to hide. The pounding inside his skull the only sound he could hear. He was just about to exit his hiding place when he heard the classroom door squeak slowly open.

Midgy froze into place, his hand reaching out towards the cupboard door. He dare not even breath, in case he gave away his hiding place. After a few menacing seconds of silence he heard the tapping of claws hitting the floor, and the ragged, deep breathing of the creature as it entered the classroom. He could only hope its sense of smell wasn't as good as that of the creatures he'd read about in horror stories.

There was a sudden crash as the creature swiped aside desks and chairs and what sounded like a roar of frustration, then silence. Midgy held his breath until stars began to appear in front of his eyes. Drawing in a much needed breath of air as quietly as he could, he heard the creature start towards the exit. He was about the draw in another breath, when a large drop of sweat fell from the bridge of his nose and landed with a plop onto the floor of the cupboard.

The creature turned at the sound and growled. Before Midgy knew what was happening, the door of the cupboard was ripped away and the entrance filled with the shining teeth of a werewolf.

Midgy let out a small squeak of terror and backed away into the corner of the cupboard. The werewolf licked its teeth and raised one massive paw slowly above its head.

At that moment Midgy saw is whole life flash before him. He didn't much like what he saw. His mum and dad had gone long ago, his gran was the only one who really cared for him. She fed him and clothed him and even gave him presents when it was his birthday. He saw her give him presents in the future and feed him his favourite jam rolly polly pudding. He saw her cry when he told her he'd got a job, and laugh when he tried to pay her from his first wage packet. He saw himself standing over her grave and dropping a blood red rose into it. He saw the bonding warehouse he worked in, full of ghosts and ghouls. He saw the school he'd studied in burning to the ground and all his friends dying in the blaze.

This was not how the world was supposed to be. He was supposed to be happy and his gran was too. Anger started to burn deep inside Midgy's stomach. It bubbled and burst, and plopped and slopped, and trembled and shook, until it grew into a ranging torrent of hate and fear. Before he knew what was happening the anger burst out of him and hit the advancing werewolf square in the chest. It was flung backwards, smashing into tables and chairs and splintering them into firewood. It hit the far wall with a thump, then slumped onto the classroom floor.

The anger inside Midgy's stomach continued to roar as he stepped out of the cupboard. It raged inside him, making his throat burn and sending icy shivers running through his veins. His vision blurred, making the room and the slumped werewolf a hazy smudge in front of him. His hair began to sizzle and his skin started to vibrate. Before he knew what was happening his bones started to break.

He let out a scream of agony and surprise as he fell to the floor. Then he began to writhe and squirm, each movement accompanied by the snapping and re-setting of bones. Midgy's eyes turned a dark black, the hair on his head and body grew and his nose sprouted out of the centre of his face. His cries turned to roars as the fingers on his hands turned into claws. After a dozen seconds that seemed to last a lifetime, most of his humanity had gone. Replaced by a snarling, angry Lycan.

The creature rose off the floor and stared at the slumped werewolf, with a mixture of hatred and expectation. It roared at the still form, then snarled and barked at it for good measure. The werewolf rose slowly from the floor, a long low growl escaping from its jaws. But the Lycan that had been Midgy could hear the fear and surprise in its growl. It was no longer the most powerful creature in the room. At that moment Midgy was the most powerful creature in the world, maybe even the universe. The building he stood in seemed small. The creature in front of him no more than a speck of dust. He knew he could wipe it away with the flick of one claw. It felt as if the whole world was too light. That it couldn't contain him and all he had to do was jump up and lift off into the universe. His universe, full of stars and gas, and planets and life. All his to command. All his to destroy or protect as he saw fit. The trillions and trillions of creatures he now saw we just ants he could crush beneath his paws. The worlds they inhabited mere pleasure domes for the Lycan he'd become. It was all beneath his contempt. He was more than a monster, more than a Lycan, he was now a God.

'You're a silly little boy sometimes Martin. You know you could never hurt a fly.'

The sound of his Gran's voice stopped the creature in its tracks. It cocked its ear, a low whine escaping from its lips.

'Remember who you are Martin. You're my special boy. You're my little helper, my bingo partner, my shopping partner. I couldn't do anything without you.'

The creature knew the voice was only in its head. But he couldn't resist the soft loving tone. It washed over him. It brought him back from the universe, brought him back from the edge of destruction. Lycan Midgy let out a howl of frustration and pain. He wasn't a God, he wasn't even a monster. He was the Knight Shift and his friends were in trouble.

The Lycan crossed the floor of the classroom in one great stride, removing the head of the snarling werewolf with a smooth swipe of its massive paw, and exiting the classroom in one breath. He raced down the small corridor, brushing plaster and posters off the walls as he went. He could hear the groans and shrieks of his friends from the other side of the school. Midgy burst through a plaster wall and out into the playground before smashing back into another building and into the dining hall. The scene was one of utter chaos. What was left of the Knight Shift had managed to barricade themselves behind a wall of tables. Midgy could see Tara cowered at the bottom, desperately trying to call the police on her mobile phone. Sarah and Tom were beating back a group of angry werewolves with broomsticks and a rolling pin, while Cameron's still form gently wept blood onto the floor. The metal smell of blood mixed with the acrid smell of fear made Midgy feel weak. He longed to taste the sweet flesh in front of him, to slake his thirst on rich, creamy blood. He took a tentative step forward, saliva dripping from his jaw and stopped as the voice in his head spoke up once again.

'They're your friends Martin, not a buffet. You're supposed to save them not eat them. Pull yourself together, they're in trouble. If you don't help them they'll all be dead. Then you'll be alone.'

Lycan Midgy shook his great head and howled. The sound full of longing and confusion.

The group of attacking werewolves stopped and turned as one. Surprise and fear splashed across their muzzles. The world seemed to stop. Sound died away, mouths closed, claws dropped and dust settled. What was left of the Knight Shift, peeked around the side of their barricade, open mouthed. The scene was held, frozen in time, and may have stayed that way if it wasn't for the silver-backed werewolf. It shook its head and roared in defiance at the imposter who stood before them. That broke the spell. Werewolves charged, Lycan Midgy charged and the Knight Shift hid.

The battle was short, and for Midgy, very sweet. Werewolves were no match for a new born Lycan. Two were dead before the silver-back's roar had finished bouncing off the walls. From behind their shelter the Knight Shift crew heard sounds of snapping bones, ripping flesh and howling werewolves. Then, after a few short, violent minutes, the hall went quiet once again.

Sarah licked her lips and tried not to breath too hard. She wasn't sure what had happened. She wasn't even sure this was real. A part of her was convinced that she'd wake up and find the whole thing had been nothing more than a horrible nightmare. But the sweat on her brow and the racing heart in her chest told her otherwise. She closed her eyes and tried to calm herself. She knew they couldn't stay where they were for long. If the new monster had decided to fight the others, this was their best chance of escape. She gripped the rolling pin she held in her hand as tight as she could and prepared to rise.

"You can come out now, they're dead."

"What!"

"I said you can come out, they're dead."

Sarah peeked out from behind the shelter and saw the most confusing sight so far. Midgy, naked as the day he was born, stood, trembling in the centre of the hall. Surrounding him were bits of werewolf. Each one slowly turning into human body parts.

"What the hell!"

"I think I killed them."

"I think you did more than that," Sarah said, trying not to vomit.

"How? I mean you weren't there Midge, there was this great big bloody dog, just like these ones. Where the hell is that? We need to go, it might come back," Tom said.

"I don't know what happened."

"It won't come back," Sarah said confidently.

"How do you know?"

"I just do. We need to get out of here." She stepped over to Midgy and gave him her jacket.

"We need to get you home."

"Yeah," he replied absently, still glassy eyed and shaking.

"We need to get him home Tom," Sarah said insistently. "The cops will be here soon and we don't want to be anywhere near the place when they arrive."

"How am I going to tell my Gran?" Midgy said, suddenly wide eyed and fearful.

"Somehow I think she'll understand."

"How can anyone ever understand this?"

"Trust me," Sarah said, as she gently pulled Midgy towards the exit. "There are more things in heaven and earth Horacio, than are dreamt of in our philosophy."

"What do you mean?"

"Nothing, just something I read. I think Mel Gibson said it once."

"Who?"

TUNNELS UNDER THE RIVER

Blaine sat in the middle of the shop, his mouth set firm, his eyes fixed on a point in the distance. He twined a piece of red coloured string around his thumb, winding it backwards and forwards, slowly making it tighter each time he wound it up.

Bob watched him through a crack in the curtain that separated the front from the back of the shop. After a few minutes he shook his head and turned towards Lewis.

"He's not happy. I've not seen him like this for ages."

"What's wrong with him?"

"No idea. He always goes quiet when he's not happy. We should avoid him for a bit."

"We can't, I need to have a chat with him about imaginary keys," Lewis said ominously.

He'd been eager to have it out with Blaine ever since he'd got back, but the creature had been avoiding him. He'd forgiven Bob, almost, he was just doing Blaine's bidding.

"Don't worry about that, we can work it out, I know of a few places we can go that will help you with the change. You'll find the thing that helps you change into a Lycan, no sweat."

"Oh yeah, you'll help me, like you did in the station. That worked out so well didn't it?"

"Look, I've already told you I wasn't to know Charlie was going to attack that guy."

"She was only defending herself. You should never have taken us to that place, it was too dangerous. You should have just told us there was no key and that we had to find the power ourselves."

"Putting you in harm's way was kind of the idea, but I've apologised for that too," Bob replied haltingly. He was still embarrassed about losing Lewis in the sewers.

"Maybe you should apologise again, I didn't hear you too well the first time!"

"I'm sorry. I thought it would be OK. I've been down there a million times and there's never been a spot of bother, and I was there to protect you."

"That just doesn't make sense. Why would you put me and Charlie in danger and then try to protect us from the very thing you've exposed us to?"

"Well we thought it would be a good trigger, that it would set you off. Kind of like having a bit of alcohol to feel good but not too much to make you drunk."

"I guess we both got really drunk then didn't we?"

"It was a bit too dangerous. But hey it all turned out OK. You met Silas and got burgers and stuff."

"After being chased through the tunnels by a pack of werewolves and only escaping with my life when Silas and his crew rescued me."

"Yeah that's odd. Why didn't you change?" Bob asked for the thousandth time.

"I have no idea, but Silas said it wasn't fear that helps me change."

"No it's not, but I have an idea what does," Blain said from the entrance way.

"Nice you could finally join us," Lewis said coldly.

"I'm sorry for not trusting you with the truth. In my defence I felt that giving you the task of finding the key would concentrate your mind and help you change more quickly."

"Well, it doesn't look like that's worked for me."

"But it did for Charlie," Bob offered helpfully.

"Shut up Bob! So what's your idea?"

"Derek," Blaine shouted over his shoulder. Derek walked into the back room, with a grin the size of the Cheshire Cat's spread across his face.

"Good evening everyone."

"Hi," Lewis replied. "Who's this?"

"Derek is going to accompany you tonight. He's new so you'll need to show him the ropes. Derek, do everything Bob and Lewis tell you. Happy hunting everyone." With that he turned and went back out to the shop.

Lewis stared at Blaine's back as he disappeared through the curtain, then shook his head.

"What is all this?"

"Plan B, welcome to the team, Derek, I hope you don't mind going on a bit of an adventure?" Bob asked with a big smile on his face.

The sewer smelt of dead rats and rubbish. But by far the worst thing about it was being down there with Derek and his verbal diarrhoea. He literally hadn't shut up from the moment they'd left the shop. His constant chatter, mainly made up of boasting about the treasures in his house and outlining in detail his expert knowledge of the Glasgow sewer system, was grating on Lewis. It took most of his effort not to turn around and punch the arrogant little man in the mouth. Why on earth Blaine had allowed him to accompany them, when he clearly didn't have a grain of magic in him, was baffling.

"I've been down this main system before you know. It goes directly under the Clyde. There's an amazing set of systems under the city and most go under the river. This one was built in 1846 as part of the city's efforts to tackle a typhoid epidemic. No doubt you know all about that from school Lewis?"

"Oh yeah, it was a big hit in history."

"Oh I'm glad of that. I do so worry about the curriculum being taught in schools these days. All this nonsense about world religions and the environment. Teach the children about their home city, that's what I say. After all they are just innocent minds ready to be filled with the wonders of social history. And take these gadgets off them, they are nothing but a corruption of the soul. It makes the little kiddies lazy and fills their heads with nonsense."

"Little kiddies!" Lewis fumed, but Derek didn't hear him, he was already onto his next lecture.

"When I was your age I read a book a week. There was no such thing as the Internet, and we were happier for it. Our minds were full of wonder and the knowledge you can find in a good encyclopaedia. None of this 'Your Tube' nonsense and all those videos of young men showing you their bottoms. What is all that about?

"Any videos of young ladies?" Bob asked with a chuckle.

"Oh I'm certain there is Bob. They have no morals you know."

They turned a corner and entered a large space with a vaulted roof. Lewis stopped in his tracks, the breath caught in his throat.

"I know this place," he said quietly.

"Did you come this way last time?"

Lewis nodded in reply.

"They're gone you know? Silas and his crew took care of them."

"Yeah but there are always more aren't there?"

"Yes and we'll take care of them when they show their ugly mugs."

"What are you two whispering about?"

"Werewolves Derek. I'm sure Mr. Blaine would have mentioned them."

"No he didn't," Derek lied, his face going white.

"Well, there are loads of them and they particularly like sewers."

"I thought we were here to look for magical creatures?" Derek asked, his voice trembling.

"And you think werewolves aren't magical?" Bob asked, laughing.

"Well I don't know, you're the experts."

"Silly me, I thought you were the expert here?" Lewis replied, his mouth full of bile. He was desperately trying not to think of the group of werewolves who'd chased him into this place only a few days ago, or the feelings of desperation and loss he felt as they chased him.

"Well of course I'm not. I have expert knowledge of many things it's true, but not magic. That's why I'm here, so you can show me. That's what you're supposed to do child. Oh I wish Cindy were here, she'd be able to explain it better to you, I was never any good with children. But she got herself killed the silly girl"

"What?" Lewis replied, his teeth grating. "How does someone get themselves killed?"

"By not listening to me that's how. We found these magical creatures and they attacked us without warning. For no reason at all. I would be dead if they hadn't gone for Cindy. What on earth would have happened to my treasures then I ask you?"

"Your treasures?" Lewis asked quietly, his attention now focussed on Derek.

"Yes my treasures! I've already told you about them, why don't young people listen? They are the greatest collection of Glasgow memorabilia ever assembled. Those idiots in the club would have taken them if anything had happened to me. Oh my goodness it doesn't bear thinking about. Nigel taking my set of railway signs, what a disaster."

"What about this Cindy of yours?"

"Like I said, they attacked her instead. More's the pity, but at least I survived." Derek replied with a sly smile.

"Oh my God, what kind of monster are you!" Lewis exploded. He'd had enough of this man, Blaine had foisted on them. His frustration finally boiled over into deep anger and it took all his remaining self-restraint not to punch Derek in the face.

"What are you talking about? I'm no monster. Cindy was a lovely girl don't get me wrong, but no great loss in the grand scheme of things. Think of the loss to Glasgow if they'd taken me. My knowledge is irreplaceable."

Something snapped inside Lewis. It was only later that he realised it had been his spine. He let out a howl of pain and frustration then fell to the ground. At first nothing seemed to happen. The world held its breath, waiting to see how he would change. Then a series of snapping noises were accompanied by a staccato of howls.

"What the hell is going on?' Derek shouted, staggering away from Lewis's thrashing body.

"At last!" Bob shouted in glee.

Lewis's world was turned upside down and inside out. He knew nothing but pain and fear. A pain so complete it shattered his mind and nearly ripped apart his soul. His whole body broke and reset itself. His arms became paws, his nose a snout, his teeth fangs. His mind reared up and tried to escape, but there was no escaping the reality of the change. A small part of him knew what was happening and welcomed it, but most of him screamed in protest. After a few moments the power took over. It surged through his body and mind. A power he had never experienced before, nor one his small human body could ever have comprehended. A power over the entire universe. He could hear the moon talking to him and distant stars singing his praises. Suns blazed for his pleasure, planets turned because he allowed it. A flick of his paw would shatter the earth into a million pieces. A nod of his head would create new worlds in its place. He knew the names of everyone living on earth and the trillions out in the universe. He could see their hopes and fears all at once. He saw Charlie and knew her fear, he saw Bob and felt his elation, he saw his mum and knew her longing. This feeling brought him back into himself. It centred him inside his new body, reminded him that he was linked to this world and always would be.

'Mum,' his mind reminded him. The word washed over him, calmed the surging power inside, resetting his mind and settling his soul.

The world came crashing in and he was back inside the tunnel, back inside the chamber, panting and growling. His paws thrashing through the brackish water underneath him.

"What the hell is this!" a tiny voice squeaked next to him. At first he thought it was a mouse, then he realised it was a human. He could smell the fear and uncertainty pouring out of it and growled at the scents.

"What are you?" the creature stammered.

Lewis looked at it with contempt. It was beneath his consideration, yet here it was, talking to him, taking up his time. Anger surged inside him and he roared at the insignificant being shaking in front of him. A chorus of roars echoed around the chamber in reply. Lewis lifted his snout to smell the feted air. The smell of werewolf hit his nostrils and he roared again, this time in glee.

The first one appeared from a dark tunnel to his left. It crouched low as it entered the chamber. Smelling its surroundings and eyeing Lewis cautiously. After a few seconds it was joined by another then another. Two more entered from a second tunnel and still more entered from a third. They spread out slowly, growls of challenge falling from their jaws.

A large werewolf with silver coloured fur was the last to enter. It was so large that it dislodged bricks as it squeezed its way into the chamber.

Lewis smiled inside. They were all dead, they just didn't know it yet.

"What is this, oh my, what is this," Derek whispered. Bob, now changed, pushed him back against a wall, roaring a warning at him to stay quiet.

The silver werewolf cleared the entrance and let out a roar of challenge. It was picked up by his companions, the sound echoing off the walls of the cavern, and ringing harshly in Derek's ears. He covered them in a desperate attempt to block out the roaring, but it did no good.

Lewis revelled in the sound. He let it wash over him like a wave. It vibrated against his bones, making his new born fangs itch in anticipation.

After a few seconds the challenge stopped echoing off the walls and faded down the tunnels. The silver coloured werewolf stepped forward and raised itself onto its hind legs. It sniffed the air in front of it then settled its gaze on Lewis.

'You are indeed of the royal blood my prince."

Lewis was shocked to hear the words reverberate inside his head and stepped back in surprise. He wasn't supposed to hear voices inside his head, and certainly not the voice of a werewolf. They were supposed to be sense-less animals, craving only flesh and blood.

'I bow to your power and dignity,' it said, lowing its head as it did. 'But you are my master's enemy and I must destroy you.'

The creature shot forward, it's paws outstretched, its jaws an open grave.

Instinct took over as Lewis casually side-stepped the on-rushing monster. With a flick of his claw he detached the werewolf's head from its body. The now separate body parts splashed down into the shallow water of the cavern. A red pool of blood slowly seeping around them.

The leaderless werewolf pack howled and snarled in anger and fear. Uncertain of what to do, a number of them recklessly attacked. Lewis despatched them easily, their corpses joining their leader in the dirty water.

The remaining creatures hovered wearily out of range. Uncertainty and fear rippling through them. Lewis let out a roar of defiance and launched himself at the werewolves. The blood lust had taken hold of him. His humanity became a small voice inside his heard, almost drowned out by the roar of blood power.

He brought down the first two werewolves as easily as a scythe cuts through wheat. Discarding their limp bodies by throwing them over his shoulder. The remaining creatures turned and ran, desperate to get away from the awesome power that faced them. One even managed to reach the tunnels and disappear inside. Lewis let out a roar of frustration and raced after the escaping creature, killing those unlucky enough to still be in the cavern as he passed them.

The tunnel was too narrow for his bulk, but he paid no attention as he rushed into the sewer. The bricks on either side gave way as he passed, bringing down an avalanche of rubble as he made his way down the tunnel.

The whole sewer shuddered as Lewis pursued his prey. Back in the cavern, Bob quickly turned back into a human and grabbed Derek, who let out a squeak of terror at the touch.

"What, what was that?" he stammered, his eyes as wide as saucers.

"That was a prince of the blood, come into his power. Time to get you out, I think you'll have to swim out if we stay any longer."

Lewis pushed aside falling masonry like it was flower petals. His anger growing as the prey continued to elude him. He turned left, then right, then rushed out into a large open sewer with a small river flowing through its centre. He leaped across it in one stride and dived into another tunnel on the opposite side. He could see his prey just out of range, and hear the fluttering of its heart. Waves of fear were flowing out of it, they smelt delicious.

He closed the gap and made a grab for his prey. The creature lurched forward at the last minute, then skidded sideways and down another tunnel. Lewis let out another roar of frustration and rushed after it.

The game of cat and mouse continued for another few turns, then the werewolf reached a dead end. Its escape blocked by a large iron gate. Despite its strength the gate wouldn't budge. It turned towards its pursuer and did something Lewis didn't expect. It changed quickly back into a quivering human.

"Please don't," he stammered, "I'm one of you, I'm a Lycan."

For a moment, the creature that was Lewis, stopped to contemplate the shivering wreck in front of it. Then he let out a roar and descended like an avalanche. It was over in seconds, the changed werewolf having no chance against the mighty power of a newly turned Lycan prince. When it was all over Lewis began to feed on his prey. The flesh was as sweet as chocolate. The creature that had been Lewis devouring it with glee. Halfway through the meal, he glanced downwards and saw that it was eating a human arm.

Waves of revulsion rushed through his body. He dropped his prey and staggered back, writhing and changing as he did. After a few seconds Lewis stood, naked, in the middle of the dirty sewer, the taste of human flesh ripe on his lips. He turned around and vomited, his mind reeling with the realisation of what he had done.

Pain and shame racked his body. He'd turned into a monster as evil as The Dark Man he was supposed to destroy. His first use of blood power was to cause death and mayhem, what kind of creature had he become?

Bob found him, sometime later, curled up in a ball, next to his prey. He wrapped a coat gently around his shivering frame and helped him up.

"The first time is always the worst mate. It'll be better next time, I promise."

"Look at what I did," Lewis managed to choke. "He said he was one of us. He said he was a Lycan."

"Oh God a blood traitor, I'm so sorry, I didn't know."

"I ate him!" Lewis spat.

"I can see that. I did the same my first time. It's the power inside. It's almost impossible to control the first time you turn. Look this wasn't you. With all that power unleashed for the first time, we're lucky you didn't split the world in half. The power is like nothing you can describe. It takes away your humanity Lewis. It makes you a monster. The trick is not to stay that way, not to become a werewolf. You did it, you came back. This isn't you my friend, I promise."

Lewis looked into Bob's eyes and saw truth in them. He wasn't use to Bob being this serious and his gravitas brought Lewis out of himself.

"You were like this too the first time?"

"Yes. I chased a werewolf half way across the highlands. I ate about half of him before I came out of it! I wasn't me the first time I changed. And when I say I wasn't me I mean it. We become another creature. We have to fight it and come back. Some don't. When I say you didn't do this I mean it, you weren't there, you'd gone away. But you came back. Now you can control it, I promise."

What Bob was saying made sense, but Lewis knew he hadn't really disappeared when he first turned. He'd become a small voice fighting the creature that raged down the tunnels. The idea that he'd mostly gone away did make him feel a little bit better though, but not much.

"I didn't know there was such things as blood traitors."

"Yeah, the lowest of the low. They know who The Dark Man really is and what he wants but they go and serve him anyway. You did him a favour."

"But why would they go over to him?"

"No one really knows. Power, revenge, no idea. Don't waste your time worrying about it, they're not worth it. Come on, let's get out of here."

They turned away from the remains of the traitor and made their way back out of the sewers and into the light.

THE ROTUNDA

Blaine stood in front of the Rotunda, and wound the piece of red string slowly around his left thumb. It bit into his flesh, making the tip turn from red to a deep purple colour. When his hand started to throb he unwound it and made his way towards the entrance.

The Rotunda had been derelict for years. Once a hub of activity, the building had been the southside entrance to two large tunnels that stretched under the Clyde. Its twin sat on the north side and was now a Chinese restaurant. Built in 1890 the round red brick building covered a deep shaft that reached down into the earth to connect with the tunnels below. Horses and carts used one tunnel while pedestrians used the other. Cars began using the connection in the 1920s, but years of car fumes had long since put off Glaswegians using it as a walkway. So had the number of people who went missing if they tried walking down the pedestrian tunnel late at night.

The whole complex was shut by the city fathers in the late 80s after a young couple and their toddler went missing one summer's evening. Now the tunnel was used by magical creatures to get from one side of the city to another.

Blaine stood inside the old hydraulic lift and listened to it squeak and squawk as it made its way down under the city. He absently wondered if Derek had ever been down here to search for treasure and concluded he almost certainly had.

He enjoyed being inside the lift, regardless of how rickety it was. He remembered when it had been installed and how proud the city had been of its new engineering marvel. Strange how time changed things, he mused. The whole idea of walkways under the Clyde had all but been forgotten now, when once it was everyone's idea of a treat. Something to enjoy with your family, somewhere to visit and feel proud of the city's achievements.

The lift came to a stop with a jolt and Blaine stepped out into the pitch black of the tunnel with confidence. He'd been here countless times before and knew what to expect. He made his way down the black tunnel, with only rats and dripping water for company. He could see ghosts of families long since dead make their way, happily down the central walkway. A young boy played with a toy boat while a little girl furiously consumed a bright red lollipop. Mums talked casually with one another, while fathers straightened their collars and prayed for the journey to finish so they could escape to the pub. Blaine smiled at the images. He'd seen them all and more over the years. He especially treasured those of the drunks and loners who'd made their way down the tunnel in the deep of night. He'd taken their souls with glee. After a few minutes of walking in pitch black he saw a small blue light up ahead. As he drew closer he saw a stationary Mr. Mono patiently waiting for him, his left arm wrapped around a pole with a lantern attached to the top.

"I didn't think you were afraid of the dark," Blaine said with a smirk.

Mono tilted his head and stared at him coldly.

"I thought you would appreciate a little light," he replied flatly.

"Very nice of you, now what do you want?"

"You know what we want."

"You can't have him."

"That's a shame, the Dark Man will not be pleased."

"I couldn't care less if he's upset, annoyed or all together put out, you can't have him."

"Then we will have to kill the girl."

"Yes, you could kill her, but what would you gain?"

"Royal blood power."

"I'm sure that will be sweet, for a while. But then what? You will have used up a source of power that would have given you much for years to come. All to satisfy your thirst. That's very short sighted. Besides, if you were just going to kill her you wouldn't need to call this meeting. So I ask again, what do you want?"

Mono smiled thinly. "You are very astute Mr. Blaine, my master is wise to be wary of you. What do we want? Simple, we want them both, so do you. We could spend the next ten years fighting each other, searching for each other's princelings, losing soldiers in the quest but that seems such a waste of time."

"Agreed, so what do you propose?"

"We will meet, in the place that is remembered. We will meet as hosts and we will fight for supremacy. The winner takes them both."

Blaine raised his eyebrows. "You would do this? Risk everything?"

"We would."

Blaine ground his teeth. He'd been waiting for centuries for The Dark Man to finally emerge from his rabbit hole. He didn't think it would be Charlie and Lewis who finally flushed him out.

"The power must be great indeed for your master to take such a risk."

"It is no risk, we will destroy you and your horde."

Blaine didn't rise to the bait. "No I don't think confidence is what motivates you. There's something special about them both. Something you're not sharing. That's very naughty of you."

"Do you agree?"

A shudder went through the tunnel, dislodging bits of brick and old mortar. Rats raced away as the ground trembled and a rumbling sound echoed down the empty chamber. Blaine smiled inside, it was just the sound he'd been waiting for.

"Yes, it will be a pleasure to finally send him back to the void."

"Your confidence will be your downfall."

"Perhaps. When shall we meet?"

"The next full moon."

"So soon? I'll look forward to it."

"I wouldn't if I was you," Mono said casually, before turning away.

"Tell him I long to meet him once again, it's been far too long," he shouted after him.

Blaine made his way back to the ancient lift with a puzzled look on his face. Why would his enemy risk his prize in this way? Why would he need both of them? The reason struck him as the lift began to rise. He nodded at the sudden knowledge and swallowed hard, the final battle was about to begin.

THE SHOP OF HIDDEN TREASURES

Lewis sat in the back of the shop and groaned. His whole body felt like it had been ripped apart and put back together in the wrong order. Every part of him ached and complained. To make matters worse his mind was in a whirl. He was repulsed by his recent actions and found it hard to come to terms with the fact that his first act as a Lycan had been to hunt down and eat another creature. At the same time he was sick with worry about Charlie. Blaine had told him what had happened as soon as he'd got back to the shop. It took both Bob and Blaine to stop him from rushing out after her there and then.

"There's nothing you can do right now. They won't be there anymore, but they will have certainly left a trap for a naive and angry young man hell bent on revenge. We can get her back Lewis but you have to trust me."

"Why should I?" Lewis spat back. "You were the one who sent her there in the first place."

"If I'd known it was a trap I would have never sent her, you have to know that. The Dark Man is clever. He anticipated what we planned and acted accordingly. He tried to destroy your school too, as revenge for us tricking him into attacking your house, he'll stop at nothing to beat us."

"Why would he try and destroy my school?"

"Because he is evil and because he can. I hear several rooms were damaged but nothing else. They were disturbed before they could do some real harm."

"So what do we do now?" Lewis asked in exasperation. He felt that nothing had gone right since their trip to the underground station and the churning in his stomach made it hard to concentrate on Blaine.

"I have been contacted by The Dark Man's representative. He proposes a battle."

"What?"

"A battle. We will met in an agreed place and fight for Charlie."

"Why would they want to do that?"

"Because they think they can win. If they do they will take you both."

"What!" Lewis said, his jaw dropping. "You agreed to this? Are you mental?"

"They will not win. Besides it's the only way we get Charlie back unharmed."

"That's idiotic! Even if we beat them, what's stopping them from killing Charlie anyway?"

"Nothing," Blaine replied with a shrug. " But they will have to bring her to the meeting place. We can take her off them."

"I like your confidence, but that's a stupid risk."

"It's our only hope. I don't know how long they will keep her alive otherwise."

"This is crazy, it's playground stuff."

"The Dark Man needs the both of you. He can't take you from this place, he knows I will protect you. He can only keep Charlie captured for so long too. Her control over her blood power is growing and will soon be more than he can contain. It makes sense that he proposes this. He wants a quick resolution and an opportunity to destroy the lycans too."

"I suppose your reasoning makes sense," Bob said. "But it's a hell of a risk."

"No it's not. They didn't hear what I did. Your power is immense Lewis. Far more that they can possibly imagine. You nearly brought down the tunnel system earlier. You will beat him. He can't keep Charlie captive and fight you at the same time."

"But he must know this too?"

"No, I don't think he does. He's so desperate to have you both he's willing to risk everything. That's his mistake and our opportunity."

"Why does he need us both? Why not kill Charlie then come after me?"

"Because the power is so much greater if he takes you together. He can't open the portal any other way."

"What portal?"

"The portal to hell of course."

"What?"

"He dreams of releasing his brothers and taking the earth. He believes he can do that if he has you both. But time is running short. Once Charlie's control grows, he won't be able to keep her captive. After that he's finished. He needs to act now. This is our chance." Blaine said the last few words through gritted teeth, his fists clenched.

"You didn't say that last time, you said he needed our power to create more werewolves."

"And he does. But he also needs it to open the portal and release his brothers onto the earth. They're demons like him. Just as powerful and just as dangerous."

"OK," Lewis said after a few moments of silence. "So what do I have to do?"

Every fibre of Calder's being was shaking. His arms shook, his legs shook, his fingers trembled and his teeth chattered. Worst of all his heart was broken in two. Blaine had called him earlier and, in that infuriating, matter of fact tone, he always used, had told him his family was dead. They'd been too late. Mono must have smelt a rat after he'd met with Calder and killed his lovely wife and two beautiful children immediately. Calder had dropped to the floor when he'd found out and wailed and screamed. He'd pulled at his hair and clothes. He'd raced around the room and punched the walls. His mind had screamed at him to attack anything and everything. He's taken out his knife and sliced the air in fury. Then he'd remembered who'd told him that his family was dead, and he made his way to the shop. He'd arrived, trembling with cold fury and stalked around the shop front waiting for Blaine to show himself. The Lycan on guard had told him Blaine was out and he needed to wait. He was sick of waiting. He wanted him to arrive so he could plunge a knife into his cold heart.

A puff of smoke appeared from behind a stack of old newspapers. Calder smiled thinly and walked towards it as it curled lazily into the air.

"You shouldn't be sleeping behind a stack of old papers boy, you'll burn the shop down." The end of a snout appeared from behind the newspapers and snorted at him.

"Oh don't be like that," Calder said, reaching out and tickling the snout playfully. The hidden creature gurgled in delight and hobbled out to get more attention. Calder chuckled, then let out a cry of pain as he remembered that his eldest had loved this creature.

"Most people mistake him for a dragon, it's funny really, he'd never hurt a fly," Blaine said, as he appeared from the back of the shop.

Calder jumped away from the drake and plunged his hand inside his pocket. Grasping the knife hidden there and squeezing the hilt hard.

"Yeah I have a lot in common with him. Most people mistake me for something other than what I really am too," he said through gritted teeth.

"What's that?"

"A man out for revenge," he shouted, pulling out the knife and launching himself at Blaine.

The creature held out its hand and Calder was stopped in his tracks. His arm held out in mid-air, his face a mask of hate and hurt. He was held like a flower encased in a glass paperweight. Unmoving and detached.

"I feel you pain my friend. You must know that? I am so sorry for your loss. Believe me when I say I would have saved them earlier if I could have. We took a risk Calder and it didn't come off. Your family paid the price. I'm more sorry than I can say. I cannot begin to understand the depths of your pain. I am sorry for it and sorry for my part in it." He stepped closer, his eyes level with Calder's. "I cannot bring your family back my friend but I can give you revenge. The Dark Man has finally shown his hand. That is thanks to you. We will meet him and beat him. You can be a part of that Calder. You can be revenged on the monster who took your family." He waved his hand and Calder's head was freed from its prison. He rolled his head around his neck, then stared intently at his jailor.

"How can you help me get revenge?" he spat.

"Do me a simple favour and it will go a long way to beating the Dark Man."

"I think I've done you enough favours over the past few days don't you?"

"I am grateful for your help, but this is not really for me. It's all part of the plan."

"What plan?"

"The plan for beating him and sending him back to hell where he belongs. Would that be revenge enough?"

Calder nodded his head in response and Blaine released the rest of his body.

"What is it you want?" he asked, rubbing his arms. His anger reduced to glowing embers inside his gut.

"I need you to look after something for me. It's a precious artefact. We're about to go into battle. If we lose I don't want this getting into the wrong hands." He handed Calder a jewel encrusted sword, that he revealed from behind his back. The weapon shone in the shop's dull light. The silver blade had writing engraved into it in a language Calder didn't recognise. The hilt was covered in green and blue gems while the pommel was topped with a deep red ruby.

"Wow, this must be worth a fortune," Calder gasped, forgetting his pain for a moment.

"More than you can possibly imagine. I have many precious things in my shop, but none compares to this. I cannot imagine it getting into his hands. I trust you Calder, that is why I am entrusting my most precious item into your care. Will you help me?"

Calder simply nodded in reply. His mind whirring as a plan began to shown itself.

"Keep it safe. You can return it to me after the battle."

"What battle?"

"The, battle my friend. We will finally meet him in open combat. One way or another this war is about to come to an end. So you see, I need to protect my things if it goes wrong for us."

"I fail to see how this helps me get revenge for my family Blaine."

"This is the most powerful artefact I own. He would give anything to have it. It has powers no being on this planet can comprehend."

"So by hiding it I'm doing what exactly?"

"You are thwarting his plans and helping me get your revenge on him."

Calder wasn't convinced, but he'd settled on his plan of action now and it started with Blaine trusting him.

"Keep it safe Calder."

"Yeah sure, you can rely on me."

Blaine gave Calder a wide smile, that sent a shiver down his spine, then turned towards the back of the shop.

"Hey, what about all your other things? I mean you've got Bottom here," he said, pointing towards the sleepy drake. "Who's going to take care of him? He's more important than some sword."

"Oh, don't worry," Blaine said over his shoulder, "that's all taken care off."

"Yeah I bet," Calder said under his breath.

THE BATTLE OF THE TWO ARMIES

Curly stood on the edge of the clearing and licked his lips. He'd been in many battles but nothing like this. An army faced him, an army of snarling beasts hell bent on destroying him. He was excited and terrified all at the same time. He could feel his comrades standing next to him and drew strength from their presence. But he was painfully aware that Zander wasn't among them. He missed her confidence. He knew they were going to miss her expertise when the battle started too. Strangely enough he realised he even missed her scowl. He would never admit it to anyone but he'd been in love with her since the first day they'd met. He knew most of his pals would find that hard to believe. Zander had never been easy to get on with, never mind like. She was a cold fish whose best side had been indifference. Everyone admired her, but love never came into it. Most of her crew would have been happy to follow her into the mouth of hell, but they would never have bought her a drink.

Curly would have. He'd have bought her several and a curry to go with them. His biggest regret was that he never found the guts to tell her how he felt. Sure, he was the wrong gender, but he who dares and all that. A big part of him hoped that the rumours of her death weren't true. He hoped he'd see her standing captive next to the werewolves, a dark scowl across her face.

"How many do you think there are?" Martine asked, breaking his reverie.

"No idea. Bet there's a lot hiding in the woods."

"Yeah, looks like bad odds."

"We've had worse, and come out on top. We can take care of a bunch of werewolves." Curly replied with a confidence he didn't feel.

"We can now we've got a secret weapon."

"What secret weapon?"

"The boy, stupid. Bob says he's got amazing power. He was there when he turned. He said he's never experienced anything like it."

"We'll see. He's new to all this. He's just as likely to attack us as he is the werewolves."

"Do you think she's gone?" Martine asked quietly.

"I don't know. If she is I bet she took loads of them out before they got her."

"That sounds like her. She'll be with Lila now. Bet they're both kicking ass in heaven."

"Yeah, complaining about the lack of decent beer no doubt," Curly said laughing.

"Can you do something for me Curly?"

"Sure, what do you need."

"If anything happens, I mean if I don't make it, can you tell my mum I love her?"

"Hang on Martine, you're going to get through this, we all are."

"You know that's not true. Some of us are done for, there's no way we're all coming out of this. Just do me this one favour, please?"

"OK, but you can tell her yourself after we've won."

"Anyone you want to send a message too?"

"Nope, oh hang on, you can tell Gral he can sing for the money I owe him."

"You and Bob both."

Bob shifted on the balls of his feet and tried to shake out the cold that was seeping into his ankles. Mist curled lazily upwards from the open expanse of ground in front of him. It spiralled into the air, over a sea of purple heather, and slowly enveloped the branches of a large oak tree that sat in the middle of the clearing. He could just make out the gathering horde of werewolves on the opposite side. The odd growl and grunt made its way over to him on clouds of thick air.

"How many do you think there are?" Guili asked.

"Enough for about three each I reckon" Fiona answered from Bob's opposite side.

"Don't worry G there's enough for everyone," Bob replied.

"Hope this doesn't take too long," Guili said, letting out a large sigh.

"Why, you got somewhere you need to be?"

"Yeah we've got that concert tonight, remember?"

"Oh yeah, I forgot about that. Hey Bob we need to leave early, you don't mind do you?" Fiona asked, a smirk on her face.

"Yeah, I'll just phone The Dark Man and ask him if he doesn't mind rapping this up quickly, I'm sure that'll be OK," Bob replied caustically.

"It's a joke, just trying to lighten the tension."

"It's not working."

Bob tightened his coat around him and left them to it.

"I think he's missing Zander." Guili said.

"We all are. Have you met the new boy yet?"

"No, I've been out hunting the past few days, have you?"

"Nope. Just wanted to know what he's like, seeing as we're risking our lives for him."

"Because we don't do that on a daily basis anyway," Guli replied, laughing.

"You know what I mean. He's supposed to be the real deal. A game changer. Blaine says he's strong enough to beat The Dark Man."

"I hope you're right, we're going to need something special to beat that lot."

Lewis sat on a log and tried to breath normally. He could feel the weight of expectation bearing down on him. His moment of truth was nearly here and he felt totally unprepared.

He still felt sick from the first change and worry about Charlie gnawed inside his gut. His body ached and his hands shook. To make matters worse his new found power gave him incredible hearing. He'd heard most of the conversations around him. They all centred on him and whether he was up to the task. Right now he wasn't sure if he was.

'I can feel your fear prince of the blood. I can smell it weeping out of you,' a voice whispered on the air.

Lewis jumped up like he'd been stung.

"Who's there?" he commanded, swirling around, looking for the source of the voice.

'Yes, I can smell your fear. I can taste your concern too. Concern for your friend Charlie. She's with me right now. Her screams are delicious.'

Lewis's stomach dropped. "I'm going to kill you," he said to the air.

'No you're going to feed me. You and your princess will feed me for an eternity.'

'It's a mistake to reveal yourself here Azazel,' Blaine said, emerging from the mist.

'Ah, Asmodeus, I wondered when you would show yourself. This is the allotted time and place. We will do battle now.'

'This is not your ground, you are exposed here. The boy could crush you with a thought.'

'We will see. I look forward to meeting you Lewis.'

"He's gone," Blaine said after a few moments of silence.

"Was that him?"

"Yes."

"I heard him in my mind didn't I?"

"Yes, he's taunting you. Do not listen to him. He hopes to weaken you before the battle begins."

"You think I could crush him with a thought?"

"This space is our ground. He risks much reaching out like that. Yes you could crush him like that. You will beat him, have faith in yourself."

"He's got her with him."

"Yes, I heard. That's exactly where we want her to be. It will take much to hold her while he battles you. It will be his undoing."

"I don't think I can do this."

"Yes, you can," Blaine replied fiercely. "You are a prince of the blood. Lycan royalty. He is nothing but a worm. Crush him beneath your feet and think nothing of it."

"What if I don't change?"

"The power is in you. It surrounds you. Call it forward and it will obey."

Lewis looked inside and knew Blaine was right. A power surged within his body he had not felt before. It was a million times more powerful than the tingling he had felt on his skin. He suddenly realised he was keeping it at bay.

It longed to be free, it longed to hunt. A warm feeling grew in Lewis's stomach and a smiled spread across his face.

"OK, let's go and say hello."

The Lycan army stepped forward out of the trees and made their way slowly across the open ground. Bob stood at their head, his hands shoved firmly inside his pockets. He could feel the anger and aggression swirling around him. It was coming off his comrades in waves.

As agreed, Lewis walked alongside him, at the front. Blaine wanted the werewolf horde to see their enemy and shiver. Curly and Martine were there too, guttural challenges coming from their chests.

They made their way slowly over the uneven boggy ground until they reached the oak tree.

"Curly, get up there and see if you can make out how many there are," Bob said.

"What am I, a monkey?"

"Just get up there."

Curly climbed the tree, grumbling as he did.

"Well?" Bob asked impatiently.

"Loads, more and more are coming out of the trees. I'd say at least three times more than us."

"Where the hell is he getting all of them from? OK everyone, time to change."

There was a series of growls, grunts, wails and howls and a multitude of lycans appeared. Lewis stood in the middle of them unfazed. He didn't want to change until the last minute. A part of him was still worried that he might not be able to, but mostly he wanted the werewolves to see him change into the monster of their nightmares.

The lycans began to move forward, slowly at first and then at a trot. A large black werewolf stepped out of the army in front of them and hurled a round object high into the air. The item twirled around in the mist and came down in front of the lycans and hit the ground with a thud. It rolled forward a few meters and came to rest with Zander's face staring at them, her mouth open, her eyes as dead as dolls eyes.

Bob howled in fury and charged forward, his comrades quickly following. Curly jumped from the tree and changed in mid-air, hitting the ground running.

Lewis stared at the severed head in horror. It was real, but his brain insisted it was a fake head, maybe even a football with a face painted on it. He could feel the rush of lycans around him as they pushed forward to attack the enemy, the wind swirling around him as they past. But he stood where he was, transfixed by the head. The slightly open mouth, the eyes with a thousand yard stare, the blood and dirt on the cheeks. It all seemed real, it had once been part of a living breathing person, but it couldn't be real. It couldn't be happening.

'Are you afraid my prince?' the voice whispered inside his head. 'Now you see what became of your friend are you afraid.'

Lewis swallowed hard and tore his gaze away from the severed head. 'No, but you should be,' he said, rushing forward.

The armies met and the sound reverberated into the air like a thunder clap. It was followed by an explosion of hate, as flesh met flesh, claw met claw and fang met fang. Martine was the first to reach the enemy. She decapitated a werewolf with one swipe of her claw, and gutted another with her fangs. Curly ripped the arms from one werewolf as it lurched forward to meet him and Fiona managed to take the legs from her first foe, before beating the next to a pulp. The fighting quickly split into mini battles between single combatants or groups of foes. Most were violent and quick, the looser adding to the body count lying across the field, the victor quickly moving onto another foe. A million sprigs of heather burst apart, creating a purple haze that floated into the air, as claws and paws churned the ground. Bodies in different states of change began to appear across the field. Their blood adding to that already seeping into the earth. Guttural snarls, howls, and cries of pain filled the heavy air, accompanied by the intermittent sound of bones snapping.

Bob weaved his way through the melee, beating a werewolf here, saving a lycan there. He grabbed one foe by the throat and hurled it into the air, grabbing it on the way down and ripping its head from its shoulders. He ducked inside a punch from another and hugged it tight. Crushing the werewolf's body against him and listening as its life force hissed out of its jaws.

A large black werewolf stood back on its hind legs and beat at a lycan with its front paws, boxing him around the face and chest before one final punch sent him to the ground.

A silver coloured werewolf with a large white stripe running down its back, snapped and bit at the legs of lycans engaged in battle, helping their foes bring them to the ground. Guili saw what it was doing and charged at it with a roar. She dived at the last minute and bowled into the larger creature, sending it crashing to the ground. Before it could recover she dived on top of it and began to rip into it with her claws.

In the mist of all the fighting a massive roar echoed across the field, sending a shiver of fear rippling through the throng. Lewis, now changed, emerged from the edge of the battle and dived into the fray, sending werewolves and lycans rattling away like bowling pins. His jaws snapped, his claws raked and werewolves fell before him. No one could stand against his power. One reckless creature dived onto his back and sunk its fangs deep into his shoulder. He shrug it off with ease and crushed its body underneath a hind paw. Another tried a frontal assault and was swotted away like an irritating fly.

The tide seemed to be drifting toward the lycans despite their inferior numbers. The awesome power of the lycan prince in their mist and their anger and hurt at Zander's death spurred them on. That was until the werewolf pack leader stepped forward. It was the size of a small truck and just as wide. A mountain of monster muscles, claws and hate. Its eyes were two hot coals, burning in the centre of its face. It roared a defiant challenge at Lewis, and bounded forward.

They met in the middle of the chaos. Connecting with such force, that the energy ricochet off them and knocked combatants close by off their legs. The monster got a swipe in first, connecting heavily with Lewis's muzzle and knocking him backwards. He hit the dirt with a loud thud, sending more violet petals into the air. The monster jumped on top of him before he could recover and began to punch his head and chest with its mighty front paws. Its jaws snapped at Lewis face, missing it by inches, but it got a head butt in that sent sparks flying across Lewis's vision. Working on instinct, Lewis brought his hind legs up and managed to push the monster off him. Sending it backwards into Guili and a werewolf, who were currently engaged in a desperate fight for survival. Lewis jumped to his feet and dived after it, bowling into its chest and sending it rattling across the muddy floor. He followed it, the blood lust now taking over. He could taste the fear deep inside the monster. It had realised that the lycan prince was the most powerful being on the battlefield and could destroy it in an instant. It got to its feet and roared a defiant challenge at Lewis, who smiled inside, this was going to be fun.

Charlie wriggled and pushed against the invisible bonds that kept her tied. She strained against them, pushing and pulling as hard as she could.

"You cannot escape my princess," the Dark Man whispered next to her. "The more you struggle the stronger I become."

Charlie ignored his whispering. She'd been with him for a few days now and he seemed to like the sound of his own voice. She let him rabbit on, while continuing to work on the bonds holding her. At first it had been like pushing against a solid wall. She'd tried to find the edges, to prise open the cracks, but she couldn't find any. It felt like she was moving her hands against a smooth pane of glass. Then, as she moved her mental hands across the mental wall, she felt a bump. She focussed on it, feeling around the edges, rubbing her mind over and over it, trying to find a weakness. After a while she detected a small flaw, a minute crack at the top of the bump. She put all her focus, all her energy, on making the flaw bigger. Pulling and pushing, making the crack bigger. Every time he spoke to her she stopped, terrified that he would realise what she was doing. She'd been working on the bump for a day now and she could feel it wobble and bend at her will. She could feel the crack was now big enough to get her mental fingers underneath, but she dare not try until her goaler was distracted. A massive battle between monsters was just what she needed. While The Dark Man had been distracted with Lewis she put her fingers underneath the crack and pulled. It came apart slowly, like chewing gum peeling off the underside of a shoe. She pulled it as much as she dared then stopped, elated at the sudden freedom she could detect in her left arm. It took all of her strength not to rip open her bonds there and then. But she knew she had to time it right in order to give Lewis as much of an opportunity as possible to beat him. She pretended to push and pull against her bonds instead, hoping he wouldn't detect what she'd done.

"Can you see my beautiful army?" he asked her. "Watch closely, it's about to destroy Asmodeus's pathetic lycans. When they are defeated, I will feast on them and take their power."

Charlie looked up and saw that the lycans were beginning to buckle under the weight of attacks, despite having a mighty prince of the blood on their side. There were simply too many of them to beat. She could see Bob standing in the middle, battling two werewolves at once.

"How did they think they could stand against me? No one can stand against my power."

There was a sudden explosion of blood and gristle in the middle of the battlefield, as Lewis ripped apart the pack leader. He stood there with blood and body parts dripping from him and roared a defiant challenge at The Dark Man. Lycans and werewolves scrambled to get out of his path while the Dark Man casually stepped forward from the werewolf line, drawing his sword with a hiss.

"You have played long enough my prince, it is time to meet your destiny."

Now the monster was totally focussed on Lewis, Charlie plunged her hand into the mental crack and pulled as hard as she could. The bonds holding her began to stretched and weaken. She could feel her other arm suddenly become free, then her left leg. Her power started to grow as the bonds weakened making her pulled harder.

'Slowly Charlie,' Blaine's voice whispered in her head. 'Wait until the last minute, wait until he is fighting Lewis.' With a effort she relaxed her mind and waited.

They met in the middle of the battlefield, the warriors around them moving away to give them space. Lewis charged first, rushing forward with his claws outstretched, jaws open wide in anticipation. The Dark Man didn't miss a stride as he stepped inside the on-rushing lycan and raked his back with the silver sword. Lewis felt a burning sensation run down the middle of his back and roared out in pain. He managed to keep his feet as he stumbled to a stop and turned quickly to see the sword rushing down to meet him. He dived backwards, the sword missing him by inches. The Dark Man kept moving forward, the sword slashing left and right as he tried to cut Lewis to pieces. Lewis danced backwards in a desperate attempt to avoid the blade, all thought of attack now gone.

They made their way through the maddening throng, werewolves and lycans melting from their path. The Dark Man never missed a beat as he attacked, his sword a whirling flash of light.

'You're strong my prince, far stronger than your princess. Even so, her blood will still taste sweet on my tongue. I have kept her breathing until now, but she will be my first meal once I have despatched you.' Lewis knew the monster was trying to provoke him, and he knew he shouldn't react, but the thought of the beast hurting Charlie sent him into a spasm of rage. He dived inside the next sword lunge and barrelled into his foe. A millisecond before impact he put all his energy into a push that sent the creature hurtling backwards. Despite the use of magic, the impact felt like hitting a brick wall, and Lewis collapsed to the floor, dazed. Martine saw him collapse and raced over to protect him. She intercepted a werewolf just as it was about to dived on top of the semi-conscious lycan. Diving onto its back, she managed to pull it away, biting deep into its shoulder as she did. The werewolf howled in pain and desperately tried to haul Martine off its back. She continued to bite, chewing down on flesh and bone until the werewolf collapsed underneath her. Without a second thought she jumped upwards and stood over Lewis's still body.

The Dark Man appeared through the crowd, walking slowly towards them. He casually loped the head off a lycan who got in front of him and took the knees from a werewolf who was pushed into him by an opponent.

Martine steeled herself for the fight and challenged her slowly approaching opponent with a series of low grumbles.

"I am impressed with your loyalty my child, but it will not help you or your prince. You will both become part me this day."

Without waiting for him to reach them, Martine rushed forward, a roar of hatred exploding from her mouth. At the last moment she dived low, avoiding the wicked blade as it shot out at her, and took the Dark Man's legs from underneath him. He barrelled over and hit the ground heavily. She scrambled to a stop and turned to charge back before he could recover, but to her surprise he was already standing there waiting for her. In that moment she knew she was doomed.

"Clever, I may even kill you quickly for that," he whispered.

Martine dug her claws into the ground and leaped forward. She only made it a few strides further before the blade took her head from her shoulders. With a sigh, The Dark Man flicked droplets of her blood from his blade and turned towards Lewis.

"It seems a shame that you are not more of an opponent. I was wrong, your princess is far more powerful, she wouldn't have been brought low so easily."

He stepped forward and raised the blade above his head. "Even so, your power will be delicious."

The lycan smashed into him before he could bring the blade down onto Lewis's exposed neck. The attack knocking the blade out of his hand and sending him hurtling backwards into the crowd. Charlie followed with a series of ferocious attacks. Punching and biting at the monster who'd dared to imprison her and kill her friends. She head butted him, bit his shoulder, smashed his arms with her massive paws and raked his face and neck with her claws. For a time she only knew hatred and anger. She only knew the enemy in front of her and the enemy had to die.

HERE COME THE GIANTS

Blaine stood on the edge of the clearing and held out his arms, a look of total bliss spread across his face. The glow of blood power surrounded him. It covered him from head to toe, enveloping him like a warm blanket. He could feel the power slowly seep into his bones. It was the first time in an age he hadn't needed to scramble about for power, or wish for a lycan to be killed so he could feed. The power seeping out of the dead bodies on the battlefield, gently floated towards him like shavings attracted to a magnet. He welcome it with open arms, feeling it fill his shrivelled soul.

'What would the power of royalty taste like?' 'Azazel must be too distracted to feed,' he thought as he gorged on the power surrounding him.

'No matter, there's enough for everyone. I might even share with him if he's nice to me.' This thought made him giggle out loud. He quickly covered his mouth, in case the fighting lycans heard him and wondered what their leader found so amusing.

'Lycans!' he cursed, inside his head. 'They've had their uses over the years, but I tire of them now. I tire of their constant squabbles and their moans. Nothing is ever good enough for them. I protect them from the humans, give them shelter and food and all I get in return is complaints. No matter there'll be far fewer of them soon and I will have eaten my fill.'

The heavier werewolf numbers were now beginning to tell. More and more lycan bodies littered the earth. Bob managed to kill yet another werewolf trying to take his head from his shoulders, but it was replaced immediately by another, who attacked him with such ferocity he was forced to retreat into the trees for a bit of protection. Guili collapsed under the weight of two werewolves attacking her at once, Fi disappeared under the bodies of her comrades and Curly was brought down by a group of werewolves attacking him from all sides. Lycans began to band together for protection and small groups started to form in the middle of the battlefield, surrounded on all sides by enemies.

Lewis, shook the dizziness from his head and got to his feet. He knew Charlie had saved him but he couldn't see her in the mayhem. If she was attacking The Dark Man on her own, she'd have no chance, he needed to find her. A group of werewolves attacked him as he began to make his way across the battlefield, but he despatched them easily. He ignored the rest of the battle, his eyes focussed on finding his friend. He saw a sudden flash of brown fur as it disappeared into the woods and rushed after it.

Fi managed to free herself from the bodies she was wedged between and, with an effort, get to her feet. The scene around her was one of total carnage. The ground was littered with pink, pale bodies, their life's blood seeping into the cold earth. Groups of combatants attacked each other ferociously, the air full of the thick sounds of fighting. She limped away from her dead comrades and tried to make her was over to Guili, who was beating off yet another werewolf attack. She didn't have the strength to defend herself and really didn't know what she was going to do when she reached her friend, but she knew she had to try. She could see small bands of lycans around her desperately fending off their werewolf opponents. It looked a doomed cause. Fi knew it was only a matter of time before they were beaten. She had to reach Guili before that happened. If she was going to die, she was going to do it standing beside her best friend.

She felt the ground shake beneath her paws and looked up to see who was charging towards her. The sight emerging from the trees made her smile, the expression looking like a grimace while she was in Lycan form. Even so she was laughing inside.

The silence amongst the trees was deafening. Lewis could suddenly hear his heart thundering in his chest and his ragged breathing whistling in and out between his jaws. The dense green foliage surrounding him was almost suffocating after the open spaces of the battlefield. It clouded his vision, making it harder to search for Charlie.

'We're here my prince, we've been waiting for you,' Dark Man's voice whispered in his mind. 'I knew you would come after your friend. Now you can die together.'

'The only one dying today is you,' Lewis said with a mental shout.

'Ahh, you still believe you can beat me, how sweet. You felt it out there on the field, I know you did. The awesome power standing against you. It was like nothing your tiny mind could ever comprehend, I know that. But don't worry, you are not the first to come up against my powers and loose. You will not be the last.'

"Kill him Lewis!" Charlie's voice echoed through the trees. He stopped and cocked his ear. The sound had come from his left. Worse it meant that Charlie was now in her weaker human form. The Dark Man had already beaten her.

"Yes, Lewis come and kill me, I'm waiting. We both are. You know where we are, come and save your friend.'

Lewis dived forward, smashing branches and bushes aside, sending a pair of nesting pigeons racing into the air and rabbits skittering out of this path. He shouldered a small tree out of his way and burst through into a clearing, where The Dark Man and Charlie stood. She was standing as still as a statue, her pale face frozen in fear. The Dark Man stood next to her, holding the sharp end of a stick at her neck. A small trickle of blood was running away from where the stick was pressed against her flesh. Lewis skidded to a halt and growled.

"Welcome Lewis I knew you would find us." It was the first time Lewis had heard the voice outside of his mind. It was just as hollow and dead as before. The sound of wind whispering through a graveyard. "So here we are, at the end time. All I need to conquer the world is right in front of me. Don't worry Lewis, don't be afraid, it's just a little death, you'll hardly notice. Once I have your blood power and mingle it with Charlie's I will be all powerful. The humans will bow before me, doesn't that thought make your skin tingle? I know it does mine."

'I'm going to end you,' Lewis replied.

"Ahhh, my prince, she can't hear you when you're a Lycan. You'll need to change if you want your princess to hear your last words."

Without thinking Lewis quickly changed back into his human form. The feeling just as weird and painful as the first time, but somehow easier now his mind was distracted.

"No! That's what he wants you to do, you can't beat him if you're a human."

"I can beat him in either form," Lewis replied through rubber like lips. He coughed and wretched, his body shivering from the change.

"That's the spirit my prince," The Dark Man taunted him. "You can beat me in any form. So come on I'm waiting."

"Let her go, it's me you want."

"Where's the fun in that? Besides I want you both. I think I'll just sever her jugular with this sharp stick and beat your brains out while she bleeds to death on the floor. Now doesn't that sound nice?"

"It sounds like the actions of a coward."

"It's the actions of demon, you stupid little boy. Your race never ceases to amaze me. What strange notions you have. Death is death. It doesn't matter how you got there, it's all the same." The Dark Man began to press the sharp stick against Charlie's soft flesh. She let out a cry of pain and pulled desperately against his hold.

Without thinking Lewis centred all his power and pushed outwards. The blast hit the Dark Man's wrist, snapping it and sending the stick flying away. Charlie pushed at the same time and the monster was sent flying into the bushes. Suddenly released from his hold, Charlie rushed forward and hugged Lewis fiercely.

"Sorry I should have stayed on the field but I thought I had him beat." she said. "I knew you'd come for me."

"Well I can't let you have all the fun. Come on let's get out of here."

"Too late."

The Dark Man stepped out of the bushes and casually flicked a leaf from his shoulder.

"Impressive. You managed to break my wrist, well done. Together you're almost unstoppable. Almost. Now it's my turn." Wind began to churn around the monster as he started to draw in his power, leaves, grass and bark swirling around the clearing.

"Get behind me," Charlie shouted, before The Dark Man released his power. The force hit them full blast but Charlie managed to erect a shield at the last minute, sending the force upward into the sky.

"You're full of surprises," the monster whispered.

"You have no idea," Charlie replied, sending her own blast hurtling towards him. The Dark Man deflected it easily and sent his own in return. This one hit Charlie low down at her ankles and toppled her to the floor.

"We could trade blows all day but what's the point? I have a world to conquer. It's time to give up your power."

"I don't think so," Lewis replied, reaching out with his mind and grabbing The Dark Man's arm. He'd remembered Blaine's words from earlier 'the boy could crush you with a thought,' and decided to test the theory.

"Do you want to arm wrestle?" the demon asked with a hollow laugh.

"No I want you to die." Lewis felt along the arm and over to the chest, plunging his mental hand deep inside. The Dark Man gasped and tried to move backwards, but Lewis grabbed hold of his heart before he could stagger back. It was a shrivelled and desperate thing. Holding it with his mind made Lewis want to vomit. He could feel it pulse underneath him like a worm trying to wriggle out of his grasp.

"No," the Dark Man whispered, holding his chest and falling to his knees.

Lewis squeezed as hard as he could, the strain making his eyes water. The heart felt like a ball of wet plasticine in his hand. It squirted between his fingers and changed shape as he squeezed. The demon gasped, then cried out, the sound echoing off the branches above them. His skin began to change colour from red, to purple then black. His eyes bulged, his cheeks puffed out and his tongue grew inside his mouth. The skin began to sizzle the more Lewis mentally squeezed his heart, the sick smell of burning flesh filling the clearing.

"Noooo," the monster moaned through a mouthful of tongue.

"Harder," Charlie whispered into his ear. "You've got him, finish him off, squeeze harder. Do it for Zander and all the others this monster's killed."

Lewis squeezed as hard as he could, his whole body shaking with the effort, his mind focussed on the shrivelled heart. He could see it in his mind's eye, pulsing and squirming beneath his fingers, desperately trying to get out of his grasp. He doubled his effort, imaging his hand was made of iron, his fingers as strong as steel, closing in on the pathetic excuse the demon had for a heart. There was a sudden popping sound as the heart finally gave way. The Dark Man screamed, an agonizing, gurgling scream of pain and fury. His body began to shake, foam flew out of his mouth, his eyes bulged out of their sockets then popped one after the other, sending blood and jelly flying around the clearing.

The monster turned into a steaming pile of flesh as his skin caught fire. He began to wriggle across the grass, leaving greasy black stains in his wake.

Lewis staggered back and fell to the floor. The effort of squeezing the heart leaving him exhausted. Charlie grabbed him underneath his arm pits and hauled him away from the dying monster.

The Dark Man raised one arm desperately towards the sky, his fingers stretch out like crooked twigs. After one more desperate gurgle he sighed and became still, the raised arm flopping uselessly down to his side. The fire suddenly intensified, giving off a blue flame that turned white hot. The flames roared like a hot furnace, the intensity growing as they consumed the monster. After a few more seconds of fizzing hot heat, the flames died down. Eventually becoming a million sparkling points of light, glowing ruby red on the tops of burnt grass stalks. All that was left of the powerful demon was a dark black stain on the ground that hissed and let off steam.

"A demon with a heart, who'd have thought it," Bob said from the side of the clearing.

"Oh, great timing Bob. Let me guess you just arrived as the monster was burning up?"

"Yes I did. I'd have helped if I'd gotten here sooner," he said, handing them both a coat. Lewis decided not to ask where he found them.

"Well you can help right now, come on he can hardly stand."

They staggered out from the trees to be met with a strange sight. A group of giants were herding the last of the werewolves into a ragged band underneath the oak tree. Silas the Satyr directing them.

"Giants?" Lewis asked.

"Yeah, looks like they finally decided which side they were on. Good news for us," Bob replied.

"It took a bit of persuading I can tell you," Calder said, emerging from behind a mound of dead bodies.

"You brought them?"

"Well no, it was Silas that approached them, but I gave him the idea."

"Yeah I bet," Bob replied laughing.

"I'm shocked at your lack of faith."

"Don't be."

"Lewis, we've never been properly introduced, my name is Calder Rough. It's nice to meet the Prince of the Blood at last."

"Likewise, haven't we met before?"

"Yes, I think we may have bumped into each other. May I have a word with you? It's quite important."

"Of course."

"In private if you don't mind?"

"You can speak in front of us Calder," Bob said.

"No I don't think so, this is private." He approached Lewis and said under his breath, "it's about your mum. I have news."

Lewis looked into Calder's eyes and knew he was telling the truth. "OK, give us a minute guys."

THE DEMON GATEKEEPER

Blaine sat on a pile of books and poured himself a steaming cup of tea. Whistling a tune about lost love as he did. He felt glorious. His whole body felt like it was glowing. His skin shined with health, his eyes sparkled and his full red lips covered newly whitened teeth. He was the picture of health for a creature older than time. A group of soldiers were chatting excitedly in the front shop but he paid them no mind. He'd fed on their enemies as well as their friends and had no interest in them anymore. Not until he grew hungry that is. Then he remembered Lewis and smiled. He wasn't going to be hungry again for a very long time. He took a sip of the steaming liquid, savouring the flavours of orange and lemon, and absently wondered what The Dark Man was feeling at that moment. Then he remembered he wasn't The Dark Man anymore. He was Azazel, one of the demon horde. Lewis had banished him back into hell, even though he probably hadn't realised what he'd done. He made a mental note to go back to the battlefield to look for the sword the creature had lost and took another sip of his tea.

"What to do with those two?" he pondered under his breath. They'd finally tapped into their powers and would only grow stronger as they practiced. He needed to control them, to channel their energies to his needs, That way he'd have an unlimited supply of blood power. But how to do it? The Dark Man had been a fool. He'd wanted to consume them. He'd become so obsessed with it he'd lost everything. Blaine wasn't that stupid. He had no intention of making the same mistake. He could wait. He could feed off them one drip at a time.

"How glorious is that going to be?" he asked himself with a smile.

He looked up to the curtain that divided him from the front of the shop and realised the soldiers had all gone quiet.

"Strange," he muttered, getting up to see what was happening.

Lewis was stood in the middle of the shop with a face like thunder. Charlie was standing next to him, her arms folded, her lips thin.

"Our mighty monarchs return," Blaine said, opening his arms in welcome.

"Where's my mum?" Lewis asked.

"Safe," Blaine replied without missing a beat.

"What about my Gran?" Charlie asked.

"Safe too."

"Liar!" Charlie screamed. "She's dead!"

There was an audible intake of breath amongst the gathered soldiers, then the room went quiet.

"Charlie," Blaine said slowly. "I was going to tell you, but I needed to find the right time."

"But you'll settle for lying to me until then is that it?" Charlie spat at him.

"You've been fighting for your lives, I didn't want to burden you with grief."

"Another lie," Lewis said calmly. "What else have you been lying to us about?"

"Nothing. I mean I haven't been lying to you about anything."

"What about blood power?"

"What about it?"

"It's your food isn't it?"

"No."

"Liar, you feed off dead people," Charlie said.

"That's not true."

"You've fed off the soldiers who died today though haven't you Blaine?" Bob asked, appearing at Lewis's side.

"I have taken their essence like I always do. I keep it safe, I remember them."

"Another lie," Lewis said. "I bet you can't remember a single one of their names. It's your food Blaine, you've been lying to everyone since the beginning. You need it to keep yourself alive. You actually need it like we need water. You're a parasite."

"No he's not," Calder said, appearing from the crowd. "He's a demon."

There was another audible intake of breath, then soldiers began to move towards Blaine.

"Wait!" he shouted. "You know me. I have been with you for a millennium. I am Blaine. I protect you against the forces of evil."

"You protect us from your opponents, nothing more. If not you then The Dark Man, if not him then some other demon. All here for the same thing, to conquer and to feed."

"And what about you Calder Rough, have I not helped you get revenge for your family?"

"Only because it suited your purpose. You're just the winning demon, that's all. You don't care for us, you only want to protect your food source, that's it."

"If that were true why haven't I enslaved any humans like The Dark Man wanted to?"

"Because you're not as mental as that monster, because you prefer to be sneaky and feed without being noticed, because you don't like their smell, I don't know and I don't care. You're a demon, you're just like he was."

"I am nothing like him."

"Another lie Blaine," Calder said. "You're everything like him, he's your brother after all."

Blaine stared at Calder with murder in his eyes.

"I know everything now, guess how I found out?"

"I can imagine."

"I bet you can. The Gatherer, he's your brother too. There are nine of them," he said to the room," Azazel is the Dark Man's real name, Asmodeus is his. The Gatherer is called Baal. All I needed to do was ask him and he spilt the beans. Oh I needed to pay him first, but the sword was worth it."

"You paid him with my sword!" Blaine screamed, moving forward to rip Calder's head from his shoulder. A dozen lycans suddenly appeared in front of him, all snarling and baying for his blood.

Calder smiled as Blaine stepped back. "Yep, a bargain as far as I'm concerned. A small price to pay for getting revenge for my family. The sword is the only thing that can bring him back from hell if someone was lucky enough to send him back to the pit where he belongs. As I said there are nine of them. All fighting to get into this world, all fighting for blood power. Blaine's had the whip hand for years. He sits on earth and does everything he can to keep his brothers in hell. This war isn't a war of wolves, it's a war of demons and it's been going on since the dawn of time. This has always been about power, the power that Blaine wants all for himself, the power to control their only food source. He lied to you about The Dark Man too. He doesn't want to open a portal into hell. He wants to control it so he can keep Blaine and he'd brothers out of this realm and keep it from himself. They're just as bad as each other. He's that greedy he doesn't even want to share you with your mum Lewis, that's why he wasn't worried when she disappeared. Now that the sword has gone we can send him back to hell where he belongs. I bet his brothers will give him a warm welcome."

"So where is she?" Lewis asked Blaine, once more.

"I have no idea," Blaine replied quietly.

"Another lie," Lewis said.

"No, this time he's telling the truth," Bob said. "You're mum was worried that Blaine was up to something, and she knew The Dark Man was after her power. She thought they were both after her, not you. She had to disappeared to protect you. She asked me to look after you. It looks like she was right. He'd be even more powerful if he got his hands on her too. I thought she was being paranoid at first, but Blaine's been acting strange for ages. Now I know why. There's been a demon in our midst all along. Strange thing is it actually suited him to have here out of the way. He wants your power and it's easier to control you and get it if your mum isn't here. Your mum isn't royalty by blood but by marriage, so she's not as powerful as you, that's why he was happy to get her out of the way. Were you going to try and fine her so you could eat her after you'd taken care of these two?"

"I mean no one any harm, you do me an injustice. I have only ever wanted to protect you all."

"So who killed my Gran?"

"The Dark Man."

"Another lie", Calder said. "You killed Charlie's Gran, and her parents before that. They probably fed you for years. You pretended she'd gone into hiding and you were keeping her safe. She took a trip to the Gatherer too and he told her the truth. Only this time I bet she tried to confront you and you ate her before she could tell anyone else. Don't deny it Blaine, you know the Gatherer doesn't lie, he said she was angry and she was going to have it out with you."

Blaine smiled and spread his hands. "She was an interfering old hag," he said. "She wanted to take away my food, I couldn't let her do that, I'm sure you understand."

Charlie screamed and dived towards him, but Bob was ready and grabbed her before she could take a single stride forward. The lycans all snarled and barked, readying themselves for the attack.

"Wait! Lewis's voice rung out around the shop, rattling the windows and shaking the pictures on the wall. "You thought to control me, you thought to feed off me, to feed off my friends and my family and then discard us when we are no further use to you. You've lied and plotted and killed at every turn. You put us all in danger just to suit your needs. You are a monster, a demon, a parasite and you deserve to die."

"But you can't kill me Lewis, I am eternal."

"No but I can send you back you hell."

Lewis shoved his mental hand deep inside Blaine's chest. The monster screamed and fell backwards clutching its chest. After a few seconds he regained his composure and began to fight back. Lewis was astonished at Blaine's strength. He could feel him grab his hand and slowly begin to push it out of his chest. He began to shake with the effort of fighting him and knew with a sudden, sickening certainty that Blaine was more powerful than him. A wicked smile suddenly appeared across Blaine's sweaty face, his perfect white teeth standing out against the violent red of his cheeks.

'You can't beat me,' Blaine's voice sounded in Lewis's mind. 'You know in the end you will lose, then what? You expect me to eat you whole? I'm not my brother, I only wish to live on this earth and protect you all from my evil siblings. That's always been my aim.'

"You're still lying Blaine, but what should I expect from a demon? You're a prince of lies.'

Lewis redoubled his efforts and began to push back against the monster. Blaine grimaced and pushed too.

'We could do this all day, but in the end you will lose, I am far too powerful, you can't beat me on your own.'

'But he's not on his own,' Charlie's voice sounded inside Lewis's head. He could feel her presence next to him, then her mental hand on his. Together they began to push.

Blaine screamed out loud as they plunged their mental hands deep into his chest and grabbed hold of his heart. It felt like an over ripe apple in Lewis's hand, his mental fingers squelching into the soft flesh. He could sense Charlie next to him, desperately trying not to gag. He focussed all his energy, all his anger, all his hate, onto squeezing as hard as he could. He knew Charlie was doing the same.

Blaine began to tremble and shake as they squeezed. Babbling nonsense tumbled from his mouth. His skin began to sizzle and a blue aura enveloped him. Steam rose from his skin and a thick, oily liquid bubbled out of his pours. Lycans coughed and howled at the smell. Most of them rushing out of the shop. Blaine's eyeballs bulged in their sockets. His face turned from that of an old man, to the pirate Lewis recognised, to a young boy and finally to a green scaled demon with red eyes and horns.

'Squeeze!' Lewis urged. 'Squeeze as hard as you can.'

'No, no, please, no,' Blaine's voice echoed inside their head. 'I'm far better than him. All I want is to feed. I can do that without hurting anyone. I don't want to conquer this world. You're far better off with me. You know the others will be coming if I'm not here.'

'They're coming anyway,' Lewis replied, squeezing harder. Suddenly he felt the heart pop, in a now familiar way. Blaine let out a roar of pain and anger and burst into bright blue flames. Just like the Dark Man, the intensity grew, the flames turning white hot, the heat pushing them back. For a moment Lewis was worried that the whole shop would go up in flames, but the heat seemed to be contained around the dying demon. After a few seconds the flames lost their intensity and died away, leaving a greasy, steaming black spot on the floor. Lewis let out a sigh of relief and staggered back to sit on the windowsill. Charlie, joining him.

"That was different," Bob said.

"Not something you see every day, I'll grant you," Calder replied.

"That was the most disgusting thing I've ever experienced," Charlie said, he face set in a grimace.

"Yeah, it's not something you'd like to do every day."

"Now what?"

"Now we find my mum, and bury your gran," Lewis replied, placing a hand on Charlie's shoulder.

"I can't believe he killed her, I trusted him."

"We all did," Bob said. "Although I seem to recall you having a healthy scepticism about him."

"He just didn't feel right. All that rubbish about finding an imaginary key"

"You got that one right."

"It was all about blood power, nothing else," Calder said. "He was desperate to keep his food supply all to himself. The Dark Man wanted to take it. But there was something else too, something I don't think Blaine knew but he did. You two are the last. There's no more royal princes or princesses after you. That's why he came out and attacked you. There's been many who've gone before you and all have been duped by Blaine and his rubbish. You two are the first to beat him."

"But he's not dead though is he?"

"No," Calder replied, shaking his head.

"So he could come back?"

"He'll certainly try, they all will, now that he's lost his place on earth. But he needs to get the sword first and I don't think that will be easy now his brother has it."

"We better get ready then," Lewis said firmly.

EPILOGUE

Mr. Mono staggered around the battlefield, the mist swirling around his feet. His dead eyes scanned the empty space around him, analysing every trampled blade of grass, scanning every dark patch of blood. The battle had been a mighty one, that much was clear. What was clearer was that they had lost and his master had been sent back to hell. For the first time in his existence Mono felt lost. The certainty that had come with serving The Dark Man was gone. A great big empty nothing was left in its place. They were supposed to conquer the world. They were supposed to beat Blaine and send him back to hell. The royal blood power giving them all the power they needed to make this world their playground. That was all gone and nothing was left in its place.

Then the sword began to call to him, pleading with him to find it, to save it, to return it to its master. Mono reacted like a drowning man given a life raft. He rushed around the field, lifting stones and ripping up clumps of grass. The voice grew louder and more urgent the closer he came to the oak tree in the middle of the field, then it stopped. Mono looked down at his feet and saw a tiny glimmer of gold, sparkling out of a clump of mud at the base of the tree. He lifted the clump carefully and the sword sang out to him as it was revealed. He grabbed the hilt and lifted it into the air, a triumphant roar bursting out of his mouth.

End of Book One

Other titles by **BLKDOG** Publishing that you may enjoy:

Arthur: Shadow of a God
By Richard Denham

King Arthur has fascinated the Western world for over a thousand years and yet we still know nothing more about him now than we did then. Layer upon layer of heroics and exploits has been piled upon him to the point where history, legend and myth have become hopelessly entangled.

In recent years, there has been a sort of scholarly consensus that 'the once and future king' was clearly some sort of Romano-British warlord, heroically stemming the tide of wave after wave of Saxon invaders after the end of Roman rule. But surprisingly, and no matter how much we enjoy this narrative, there is actually next-to-nothing solid to support this theory except the wishful thinking of understandably bitter contemporaries. The sources and scholarship used to support the 'real Arthur' are as much tentative guesswork and pushing 'evidence' to the extreme to fit in with this version as anything involving magic swords, wizards and dragons. Even Archaeology remains silent. Arthur is, and always has been, the square peg that refuses to fit neatly into the historians round hole.

Arthur: Shadow of a God gives a fascinating overview of Britain's lost hero and casts a light over an often-overlooked and somewhat inconvenient truth; Arthur was almost certainly not a man at all, but a god. He is linked inextricably to the world of Celtic folklore and Druidic traditions. Whereas tyrants like Nero and Caligula were men who fancied themselves gods; is it not possible that Arthur was a god we have turned into a man? Perhaps then there is a truth here. Arthur, 'The King under the Mountain'; sleeping until his return will never return, after all, because he doesn't need to. Arthur the god never left in the first place and remains as popular today as he ever was. His legend echoes in stories, films and games that are every bit as imaginative and fanciful as that which the minds of talented bards such as Taliesin and Aneirin came up with when the mists of the 'dark ages' still swirled over Britain – and perhaps that is a good thing after all, most at home in the imaginations of children and adults alike – being the Arthur his believers want him to be.

**A Storm of Magic
By Ashley Laino**

Being brought back from the dead is an impressive trick, even for magician Darien Burron. Now he must try and use his sleight of hand to swindle modern-day witch, Mirah, to sign her power away, or end up a tormented demon in the afterlife.

Meanwhile, sixteen-year-old Mirah is starting to lose control of her powers. After an incident at her aunt's Witchery store, Mirah is sent to a secret coven to learn to control her abilities. While away, Mirah meets up with a soft-spoken clairvoyant, a brazen storm witch, and the creator of dark magic itself. The young woman must learn to trust in herself before she loses herself entirely to the darkness that hunts her.

Weirder War Two
By Richard Denham & Michael Jecks

Did a Warner Bros. cartoon prophesize the use of the atom bomb? Did the Allies really plan to use stink bombs on the enemy? Why did the Nazis make their own version of Titanic and why were polar bear photographs appearing throughout Europe?

The Second World War was the bloodiest of all wars. Mass armies of men trudged, flew or rode from battlefields as far away as North Africa to central Europe, from India to Burma, from the Philippines to the borders of Japan. It saw the first aircraft carrier sea battle, and the indiscriminate use of terror against civilian populations in ways not seen since the Thirty Years War. Nuclear and incendiary bombs erased entire cities. V weapons brought new horror from the skies: the V1 with their hideous grumbling engines, the V2 with sudden, unexpected death. People were systematically starved: in Britain food had to be rationed because of the stranglehold of U-Boats, while in Holland the German blockage of food and fuel saw 30,000 die of starvation in the winter of 1944/5. It was a catastrophe for millions.

At a time of such enormous crisis, scientists sought ever more inventive weapons, or devices to help halt the war. Civilians were involved as never before, with women taking up new trades, proving themselves as capable as their male predecessors whether in the factories or the fields.

The stories in this book are of courage, of ingenuity, of hilarity in some cases, or of great sadness, but they are all thought-provoking - and rather weird. So whether you are interested in the last Polish cavalry charge, the Blackout Ripper, Dada, or Ghandi's attempt to stop the bloodshed, welcome to the Weirder War Two!

Click Bait
By Gillian Philip

A funny joke's a funny joke. Eddie Doolan doesn't think twice about adapting it to fit a tragic local news story and posting it on social media.

It's less of a joke when his drunken post goes viral. It stops being funny altogether when Eddie ends up jobless, friendless and ostracized by the whole town of Langburn. This isn't how he wanted to achieve fame.

Under siege from the press, and facing charges not just for the joke but for a history of abusive behavior on the internet, Eddie grows increasingly paranoid and desperate. The only people still speaking to him are Crow, a neglected kid who relies on Eddie for food and company, and Sid, the local gamekeeper's granddaughter. It's Sid who offers Eddie a refuge and an understanding ear.

But she also offers him an illegal shotgun - and as Eddie's life spirals downwards, and his efforts at redemption are thwarted at every turn, the gun starts to look like the answer to all his problems.

Burning Bridges
By Chris Bedell

They've always said that three's a crowd...

24-year-old Sasha didn't anticipate her identical twin Riley killing herself upon their reconciliation after years of estrangement. But Sasha senses an opportunity and assumes Riley's identity so she can escape her old life.

Playing Riley isn't without complications, though. Riley's had a strained relationship with her wife and stepson so Sasha must do whatever she can to make her newfound family love and accept her. If Sasha's arrangement ends, then she'll have nothing protecting her from her past. However, when one of Sasha's former clients tracks her down, Sasha must choose between her new life and the only person who cared about her.

But things are about to become even more complicated, as a third sister, Katrina, enters the scene...

**Father of Storms
By Dean Jones**

Imagine losing everything you loved as well as the future you'd wished for so long to come true.

Seth was born with the gift to manipulate energy, unfortunately his skills mark him as a target for one who wishes to control everything. So began a life running from those who would seek to command him, a life that spans over a thousand years waiting for the day when all will be once again as it was.

Captured in modern day London, Seth needs the help of his companions, the Mara, to show him who he is through dreams of his past, so he can save the family he has waited so long to have. A warrior bred for battle must fight once more but this time the battlefield is his mind. Can Seth win, or will he finally lose who he is and become the weapon of the man who started his nightmare all those years ago? *Father of Storms* is a story told through time, a tale of love and hope where there seems to be none and above all it is a reminder that if you believe, truly believe then even from the darkest places, good things come to those who wait.

www.blkdogpublishing.com